DRONE ACADEMY

SWARM

MATTHEW K. MANNING

Capstone Young Readers
a capstone imprint

Drone Academy is published by Capstone Young Readers,
A Capstone Imprint
1710 Roe Crest Drive
North Mankato, Minnesota 56003
www.mycapstone.com

Library of Congress Cataloging-in-Publication Data is
available on the Library of Congress website.

ISBN: 978-1-62370-992-1 (paperback)

Summary: Four full-length stories featuring the members of
Drone Academy, a team of anonymous, virtual-reality-wearing
teens who communicate exclusively in cyberspace and interact
only through their high-tech UAVs.

Designer: Aruna Rangarajan
Cover illustration by Allen Douglas

Elements: Shutterstock: andrewvect, (banner) cover, Prazis
Images, (city) cover, Reinke Fox, (drones) cover, Rost9,
(pattern) design element, Supphachai Salaeman, (screen)
design element, TRONIN ANDREI, (drones) design element,
WindVector, (video) design element

Printed and bound in China.
010737S18

THE MISSIONS

THE SWARM TEAM

Zor_elle

Name: Zora Michaels

Age: 16

Ethnicity: African-American

Home base: Rural Indiana

Interests: As far as her classmates know, fashion, trends, and the coolest clothes and accessories; in reality, science, computers, comic books, and SWARM; all things pink

Drone: The Beast — the largest drone on the SWARM team; several feet wide with four industrial gray helicopter blades and a black, crane-like camera; camouflage colors help it blend into its surroundings

HowTo

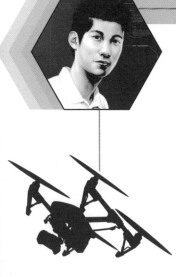

Name: Howard To

Age: 16

Ethnicity: Vietnamese-American

Home base: Los Angeles, California

Interests: Science fiction, comic books, and all things fantasy — everything from movies starring trolls and elves to role-playing games featuring wizards and warlocks

Drone: Redbird — the sleekest and flashiest of all the SWARM drones; a slick, red hot rod with four black helicopter blades, shiny red paint, red and yellow painted flames on the sides, and a small black camera in its center

ParkourSisters

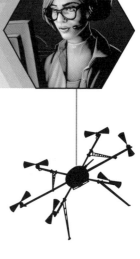

Name: Parker Reading

Age: 16

Ethnicity: Caucasian

Home base: New York, New York

Interests: Athletics, specifically wrestling and martial arts; computer hacking — and using her computer skills for the good of SWARM

Drone: Hacker — a small gray drone, almost bug-like in appearance; Hacker has red and green lights and six helicopter blades; the most technologically advanced drone in SWARM's arsenal

saiguy

Name: Sai Patel

Age: 15

Ethnicity: Indian-American

Home base: Savannah, Georgia

Interests: SWARM logo design; a founding member of SWARM

Drone: Solo — the smallest of the SWARM drones; bright white with four blades; a guard bar around the drone's exterior protects those blades while a harness in the center carries Sai's smartphone

USER PROFILE

INVISIBLE MODE

CHAPTER 1

BEHIND THE PINK DOOR

"So you heard why Jessica can't go, right?" Gabby said from behind the wheel of her tiny red Toyota as she rolled through a stop sign on Second Avenue.

Zora Michaels glanced over at her friend, studying Gabby's long, dark hair and pretty features. Up until that point, Zora hadn't really been listening. She'd been distracted, looking out the window, watching the familiar front yards pass by. But hearing Jessica's name snapped her back to reality.

"No," Zora said. "Why?"

"She said she's — and I'm quoting here — 'got to spend the day studying for the PSAT.' Can you believe that? How is that more fun than cheerleading tryouts?"

"Well, getting ready for college is pretty impor—"

"I know, right?" Gabby interrupted. "I mean, we have the rest of our lives to be all studious and serious. Live it up while you can, you know?"

Zora didn't respond. Cheerleading was far from her favorite topic — not that she could tell her friend that. Gabby would never understand. Instead, Zora went back to looking out the window.

Gabby turned her car onto Pine Street. Zora was almost home.

"You at least have a good excuse," Gabby said.

"Yep," said Zora. "Can't miss my dentist appointment. Plus I told Mom last week I'd go shopping with her."

"Ugh, you're so lucky. My mom's idea of shopping is raiding my sister's closet. Everything in there is like five years out of style."

Gabby pulled up in front of Zora's house and flipped down the visor above her head as soon as the car was in park. She pushed her bangs out of her eyes and checked her lipstick in the mirror. It seemed to meet her approval, but just barely.

"Well, have fun at tryouts." Zora smiled, trying to look genuine, and pushed her door open. She straightened up and brushed her curly black hair off her shoulder, then flung her bag over her shoulder.

"It'd be more fun if you were there," said Gabby, thumping the visor back in place.

"Wouldn't everything?" Zora replied. She smiled again before turning to walk away.

"You wish!" Gabby called. She pulled away from the curb with an accidental lurch, as if having trouble with the clutch. Interestingly enough, her car was an automatic.

Zora shook her head as she pushed her key into the front door's lock. Another day, another invite to something she didn't care about. She had better things to do than stand by the sidelines at games she had no real interest in, shouting encouragement for athletic feats she wasn't all that impressed by.

The situation did present an interesting challenge, though. Now Zora had to come up with a week's worth of excuses to miss out on cheerleading tryouts. That was the only way to get out of the coming season.

The door creaked open, and Zora stepped inside and out of her black boots. As she walked up the stairs, she felt the plush white carpet on her toes, even through the material of her knee-high socks. At the top of the stairs she saw the familiar kitten poster plastered on her pink bedroom door. The little cat was still hanging from its branch. So determined. An inspiration, really.

Inside, a familiar world of pink waited for her. Pink walls. Pink bed sheets. Even a pink beanbag chair. She closed the door behind her. Then, as quietly as possible, she turned the lock and rushed over to her laptop — pink, of course — to power it on.

As her computer booted up, Zora placed her pink headset over one ear, pulling the mic in front of her chin.

"Launch," she whispered. With that, she let out a low, relieved breath. The show was over. She could finally be herself. She was home.

Zora glanced out the window, past the reflective foil flower sticker and the stuffed cat with suction cup paws. She had a perfect view of the attached garage. As she watched, the octagon window sprang open, thanks to her custom automated smart hinges. Then the machine reared its ugly head — the Beast.

The drone was hefty, earning its name on appearance alone. It was bigger than the ones piloted by her friends, probably twice the size of its nearest competitor. With four gray, industrial-looking blades, a camouflage-painted hull, and a black crane camera, the Beast looked like a futuristic sci-fi prop brought to life.

The Beast was everything Zora hid from the world. The Beast was her better half.

"Where you been, Zor_elle?" a voice in Zora's ear asked. It was Howard To, a fellow SWARM member and probably Zora's closest friend in the whole group.

"School," she answered.

"Eh. I think it's overrated," Howard said. "Patch me in?"

"Get your own drone," Zora said.

"Aw, come on! You know I'm replacing the camera on mine. He won't be up and running until next week."

"You're such a moocher," Zora said. "Hold on."

Her fingers skimmed over her keyboard with lightning-fast speed. The screen on her laptop jumped from page to page, finally pausing when a password box popped up, front and center.

Zora typed in *Zor_elle* for the name. In the password box, she typed a series of thirteen seemingly random letters and numbers, a mixed batch of upper and lowercase. She knew better than to use a word or a common phrase for her passcode and memorized a new sequence every week to keep hackers at bay.

A website opened on Zora's screen. The words *Drone Academy* were written across the top of the page, made to look like the logo of a college or university.

Zora checked the message board record. There were only two active users at the moment, including Zora. Half the approved members of the current team. The community had been larger just a few months ago, but things had changed. Security was now more important than ever, and the club had become as exclusive as possible.

The club. Zora smiled when she thought those words. Sure, they were a club, but they were also something more. A squad. A unit. They were SWARM, the Society for Web-Operated Aerial Robotic Missions. And she was a founding member.

Zora clicked on Howard's username, HowTo, then clicked on the video icon. She typed a bit of code into the message box that appeared and pressed enter. Suddenly, the live feed from her drone appeared over instant message.

"All right," Howard said in her ear. "Where to today?"

"Anywhere but here," Zora said.

"I like it," Howard said. "That's my favorite place."

CHAPTER 2

HOBEY HALL'S GREAT ESCAPE

Hobey Hall was sick of brushing his teeth. He was sick of taking the trash cans downstairs every Wednesday night, and he was sick of walking his dishes to the counter after every single meal. He was sick of not being able to watch cartoons before school. He was sick *of* school. He was sick of his older sister coming into his room and taking his reading light. He was sick of the neighbors' dog barking a half hour before the sun came up. He was sick of his stupid room in his stupid house.

Hobey Hall was sick of everything.

Last night he'd packed his bag without anyone in his family noticing. He'd made a week's worth of peanut-butter-and-honey sandwiches, swiped a couple bananas from the counter, and filled his water bottle. He'd grabbed his tablet for something to do and an extra sweatshirt in case it got cold at night. He'd even packed his favorite truck — the red one with the lightning bolt on the side.

Hobey was ready for anything. All that was left to do was to sneak out.

He'd been awake for more than an hour now. By the time the neighbors' dog had started barking, Hobey was dressed and ready to go. In about fifteen minutes, his mom would come into his room and tell him to get ready for school. But in fifteen minutes, Hobey would already be gone.

He zipped up his sweatshirt and pulled the hood up over his head. Usually Hobey didn't wear his hood, but anyone who was up to something on TV always wore their hood up. It looked sneakier that way. And Hobey was certainly up to something. He was about to attempt the world's greatest escape.

The door didn't make a sound as Hobey eased it open. He peered out into the hall with one eye, then the other, then with his whole head. His parents were still asleep, ignoring the dog as usual.

Only the balls of his feet touched the hardwood floor as Hobey tiptoed down the hall and into the kitchen. He shoved one foot into a sneaker, then the other, nearly falling over in the process. Luckily, he managed to keep his balance and was soon at the back door.

Hobey took one last look around inside his house. It was dark and still. The well-worn leather couch sat empty in front of the television, waiting for someone to flop down onto it. But that someone wouldn't be Hobey. Not ever again.

Hobey felt something like a lump in his throat as he realized he wouldn't be back. But he had made up his mind. This place wasn't for him. No one ever listened to him here. He never got to do what *he* wanted to do. Everyone just saw him as the baby, and he was sick of it.

From now on, Hobey was going to live out in the woods behind the park. He would be like the cavemen he'd read about at school, or like Tarzan. He'd be like those guys on the survival shows on TV. He would live off the land. And no one would ever make him brush his teeth again.

He opened the back door and slipped out, making sure to lock it tightly behind him. And with just three steps down the front porch to the sidewalk, Hobey Hall had run away from home.

CHAPTER 3

ALL BEFORE COFFEE

The semi-truck came to a stop along the side of the highway. Its owner, Burt Fenton, stretched as he stepped from its cab. He'd been driving all night, and he was still a good three hours from home. He knew he should stop for the evening. Call it quits and take a nap in the small bed behind his seat. But he was *so* close to being finished with his trip. He just needed to grab a cup of coffee at the next rest stop. More than that, he needed some fresh air.

Burt walked around his truck, cracking his neck as he rotated it. There was a chill outside. Just enough to keep the dew on the grass. It was the last gasp of the cold night before the sun came up, any second now. He kicked his truck's front left tire, more out of habit than anything else. But his foot didn't bounce back as quickly as it should have. The tire felt low, maybe dangerously so.

Burt bent down and examined the tire, but he couldn't see that anything was wrong. This stretch of highway was dimly lit, which didn't help. There were no overhead lampposts, and the sun seemed to be sleeping in.

With a sigh, Burt climbed up the passenger side, opened the door, and popped the glove compartment. Without looking, he shoved his hand inside, feeling for the flashlight his wife had bought him last Christmas. Instead, he came back with a memento from an earlier time — his cigarette lighter.

Burt had given up smoking more than three years ago. It was a disgusting habit, one he'd taken up after high school. A dumb decision made by a dumb kid pressured by other dumb kids. He'd finally broken the habit, but it was one of the hardest things he'd ever done. Still, he kept the lighter around. It had been given to him by his grandfather. A souvenir from World War II. That lighter represented the dumbest part of Burt Fenton's life, but it also represented the most heroic part of his grandfather's life.

Burt smiled as he brought the lighter in front of his face. Looks like he had another job for it.

He shook the old thing open and flicked it until it glowed with a faint flame. Then he lowered it in front of the tire. It took him a good sixty seconds to find the first nail, then another three seconds to find the second one.

He'd have to get to that gas station quicker than he'd originally planned, Burt realized. He would replace the tire and grab that coffee . . . maybe even a candy bar or two.

Meanwhile, the lighter kept burning. Lost in thought, Burt Fenton inched his thumb too close to the still-burning flame.

"Ah!" he yelled as it singed his skin.

Instinctively, Burt tossed the lighter away into the nearby bushes, instantly regretting his actions. He started for the bushes but tripped over something in the grass. Hitting the ground, he let out a sound somewhere between a curse and nonsense. Then he stood up and cringed. That fall would hurt tomorrow.

Burt looked over to the bushes. No sign of light, which meant the flame was probably extinguished. The fall had likely knocked the lighter's lid back on.

He had two choices now. He could go spend the better part of an hour digging for his grandfather's old heirloom, a nearly worthless piece of metal he kept around for sentimental reasons. Or he could hop back in the cab, start toward that gas station, and get on with repairing his tire. And better yet, get to sipping that coffee.

With a sigh, Burt walked around the front of his semi and climbed up to the cab. He turned his key in the ignition. And without another glance, Burt Fenton drove away.

Meanwhile, in the bushes, a small plume of smoke began to snake its way up toward the rising sun.

CHAPTER 4

THE QUIET NOISE

Something was up at Freepoint High. Gabby wasn't waiting for Zora outside the school's front door when her bus arrived. Kim and Kate, the Kabulski twins, weren't rearranging their locker decorations in the sophomore hall for the six hundredth time this month. The Jessicas weren't gabbing near the stairwell next to the gymnasium. No one was at his or her usual station, and it was starting to freak Zora out.

The halls seemed quieter than usual too. Kids were talking but in whispered tones. No jocks were roughhousing, no goths were mocking them, no nerds were avoiding them. It was almost like someone had died. It was *that* quiet.

Zora hurried into homeroom to see Gabby and one of the Jessicas looking over at LeAnn Hall. That in and of itself was odd. LeAnn Hall was certainly not on the Jessicas' radar. She was one of the Lab Rats, the kids who stayed after school to design websites and program code in Mr. Reach's computer lab.

Although they barely spoke these days, Zora knew LeAnn better than her current group of friends realized. Back when they'd been kids, before things had changed, they'd been nearly inseparable. Zora had always admired LeAnn's ability to just be the person she wanted to be. LeAnn didn't care about fashion or about what the fashionable girls thought of her. That attitude hadn't won her many friends, but it was refreshing. It was honest. It was the exact opposite of Zora's life.

While Zora was busy spending all the money she earned from teaching piano on clothing she didn't really like, need, or even want, LeAnn was geeking out about the latest software or graphic design trend. But Zora had an image to maintain. It was hard enough being one of the only girls with brown skin in a sea of pale Midwestern kids, not to mention one who loved science and computers.

Every time she was introduced to someone new, Zora could tell what was on their minds. Her ethnicity was there like an elephant in the room. Finally, someone would say, "Where are you from?" and Zora would say, "Here" in response.

It was true. She'd lived in rural Indiana her entire life. But that didn't stop the suspicious looks from older people when she was shopping. It didn't stop her from standing out at Freeport, which had almost no diversity. It didn't stop the fascination some of the girls at school had with her hair.

But Zora was outgoing. Zora was friendly. And Zora was funny.

She had lucked into hanging out with the cool kids way back in third grade and had never looked back. Now she got to sit at the long table at school and roll her eyes at even the most popular boys. She found a way to fit in, even if it meant losing her friendship with LeAnn. Even if it meant pretending. Because fitting in was everything in high school. It was survival.

Zora watched as LeAnn cried at her desk. She couldn't trade all of that for LeAnn's quiet, brave little life.

But LeAnn's world was hardly quiet now. It was loud — the kind of loud that no one wanted.

At her side, Ellen Miller was on tissue duty. Mrs. Randall stood on her other side, lightly patting LeAnn's back as if she didn't know what else to do. Every eyeball in the classroom was fixed on the scene. Something bad had clearly happened.

"It's her brother," Gabby whispered when Zora was within earshot. "He's dead."

"He's not dead!" Jessica with the short hair whispered. "Jeez, Gabby."

"Other Jessica told me he was dead!" Gabby whispered back, returning short-haired Jessica's harsh tone.

"Well, other Jessica is an idiot," said short-haired Jessica.

"What happened?" Zora asked. Her whisper was noticeably more polite.

"I guess he went out last night — or this morning. They don't know. He, like, ran away," whispered short-haired Jessica.

"Yeah, and he might be dead," said Gabby, speaking too loudly.

LeAnn looked up from her seat in the corner of the room. Her face was emotionless. Zora couldn't tell if she was desperate or angry. Short-haired Jessica elbowed Gabby in the ribs. Then she took Zora by the hand and led her out of the room. An annoyed Gabby followed after a second or two of quiet outrage.

"So you're having trouble with your allergies, I'm guessing," said short-haired Jessica now that she was free to talk at full volume.

"Well, yeah," said Zora, not understanding. "What's your point?"

"The smoke — you can't go outside and not notice it," said short-haired Jessica.

"What?" Zora said.

"There's a forest fire. It's all over the news," said Jessica. "Haven't you at least seen it on social media?"

Zora did her best to keep her poker face. She hadn't been on any of her social media accounts in days. Unless you counted the many hours she'd spent on the SWARM message boards. But the other girls didn't know about that part of Zora's life, and she had no intention of sharing it. Piloting drones on secret missions wasn't quite "on trend."

"The fire is over by the woods near Whitman Park," said Gabby. "That's close to where LeAnn lives."

Zora was about to respond, but her lips tightened together instead.

"So in other words," Gabby said, "it's a bad time to run away from home, if that's even what —"

"I don't feel good," Zora said, interrupting whatever Gabby was about to say. She had to get out of there. She had to *do* something. "Tell Mrs. Randall I think I'm going to throw up, and I went home."

"Wait," said Jessica, calling after Zora, now almost an entire hall length away from her and still sprinting in the opposite direction. "You need to tell the office!"

But Zora didn't hear her. She'd already left. School would have to wait. A little boy was in danger, and for once, she was in a position to help.

CHAPTER 5

THE FORT IN THE WOODS

There was no smoke at seven in the morning when Hobey Hall walked through Whitman Park. He didn't smell anything out of the ordinary when he squeezed between the uneven wooden rungs of the fence that lined the Danbury property.

To be fair, Hobey didn't know the woods belonged to the Danbury family. He didn't even know the Danbury family existed. He only knew the large, sixty-acre woods as an extension of Whitman Park.

But by the time Hobey walked farther into the woods, he was beginning to think he might have made the wrong choice. Because there was no denying it — the forest smelled like smoke.

It had to be a bonfire or something, Hobey told himself. Maybe someone burning leaves or roasting hot dogs. It didn't seem odd to him that someone would be cooking hot dogs at seven in the morning. He was too caught up in his mission — getting so far away from home that his family would never find him again.

But to do that, he'd have to keep going. He'd have to find the deepest and darkest part of the woods. A place where he couldn't hear the cars on the highway or kids playing at the park. He'd have to get so deep into the forest that the world became a different place altogether. It would be like how things were back in the caveman days — no cars or phones or toothbrushes or toilets or even, sadly, video games.

But Hobey was prepared. He had brought snacks, after all.

After an hour or two — it was hard to tell time in the woods — Hobey decided he had walked enough. His shoes were a bit too tight, and they rubbed at the heel. So when he found a rock formation, one that had a beam of sun hitting it just right near the top, he decided to set up camp.

There were three big rocks altogether. Two seemed to lean on each other, pushing together like each was hoping to knock the other down. The third rock lay on the ground before the other two and was about half as high as the pair of six-foot boulders. It was the perfect oversized stepping stone for Hobey, though, and he did his best to climb on top of it.

His muddy, dew-covered shoes slipped once. But after scraping his shin so lightly he didn't even notice, Hobey managed to scramble to the top of the lower boulder. With a small jump, he landed on one of the leaning boulders. A quick, yet valiant, struggle followed, and Hobey managed to use all his might to push himself up and conquer this mini mountain.

The sun was brilliant, and the goose bumps Hobey had acquired during his walk through the woods quickly disappeared. He dangled his legs over the edge of the boulder and leaned back. He laced his fingers together, rested his head in his palms, and closed his eyes.

He felt happy. This was the life Hobey had wanted. But there was still that lingering smell of smoke. He'd be very glad when that neighbor finished cooking his hot dogs or burning his leaf pile.

Hobey sat up and unzipped his backpack. It was time for a snack. He grabbed a banana, unpeeled the greenish-yellow peel, and took a big bite. It wasn't quite ripe enough, but he knew from what he'd seen on TV that he would need to keep his strength up if he was going to survive in the wild. That meant eating the whole banana. Because next on his to-do list was building a shelter.

The only snag was that Hobey had no idea how to go about building a shelter. He'd built several forts in his life, but they'd all been made of blankets, sheets, and pillows. But still, how hard could it be to construct the same sort of things out of branches and leaves?

As it turned out, very. It was very hard to construct a fort out of branches and leaves.

It took a good forty-five minutes, but Hobey managed to drag over two large tree branches and prop them up against the sunniest side of the rock formation. His structure looked nothing like the big natural cabin he'd pictured while drifting off to sleep the past week. His creation looked more like a pile of twigs constructed by a lazy beaver.

It'll have to do for now, Hobey thought. He could always make it better later. He filled the shelter with dry brown leaves to serve as padding and then crawled inside. The shelter was OK, but it still needed something to make it feel like home.

Then the idea came to him — every good fort needed a flag. Hobey crawled out of his creation once more, found his backpack nearby, and retrieved his extra sweatshirt. It was bright blue. Then he grabbed the longest stick he could find and hung the sweatshirt by its hood from the stick's end.

With all his might, Hobey shoved the stick into the ground at the base of his fort. Just like that, his new home had a flag. Anyone who accidentally chanced upon this section of the woods would know that this land had been claimed. This land, these rocks, this fort — it was all Hobey's now. The flag proved it.

Hobey crawled back in his fort and flipped onto his back. The two tree branches and their leaves leaned just a foot or so above his head. He pulled his hood out from under his back and bunched it behind his head. Combined with a nice scoop of dry leaves underneath, it made a fine pillow.

Hobey closed his eyes. The TV had said that survival in the wild meant conserving your energy. A nap was in order.

As he started to nod off, he noticed the faint smell of smoke again. It almost seemed to be getting stronger. But soon Hobey was asleep, and smell wasn't an issue.

CHAPTER 6

WAKING THE BEAST

It took Zora fifteen minutes to run all the way home. That included the two minutes she stopped to catch her breath outside Fisher's Convenience Store. She'd lost her breath again by the time she unlocked the front door to her house, but that didn't stop her from running up the stairs.

She logged onto her computer and onto the SWARM website. Almost instantly, an IM popped up on her screen.

HowTo: *What up, Zor_elle?*

For a minute, Zora was confused. Shouldn't Howard be in school? But then she remembered that he was based in California. There was a three-hour time difference.

Hey, she typed in response.

Playing hooky, huh? Howard wrote. *You're turning into me.*

Zor_elle: *I wish. There's a problem. A little boy ran away from home.*

HowTo: *And you're trying to find him with the Beast?*

Zor_elle: *Before a forest fire does, yeah.*

Whoa! That's nuts! Howard typed. *Patch me into your headset so you can free up your hands.*

Zora did as requested. Howard was one of the few SWARM members she spoke to outside of IM'ing. He was one of her only friends who really got *her*. He'd gotten the joke — a play on Supergirl's real name — right away when he read her screen name. The two shared a love of comic books, a topic Zora could never discuss with her school friends. Howard was a fan of all things sci-fi and fantasy. He loved any reality that took him away from his daily life.

Zora couldn't imagine wanting to escape California. Indiana, sure. That made sense. Her life here was schoolwork and cornfields. Howard was next to the ocean. He had Los Angeles in his backyard. But to hear him tell it, his life was as mundane on the West Coast as hers was in the Midwest. Comic books and drones got them both through days that would have otherwise bored them to tears.

"Launch," Zora said into her pink headset. An instant later, the Beast's hulking figure lurched forward out of her garage's secret exit.

"So," said Howard into her ear, "you know where the kid is?" His voice wasn't lighthearted and jokey as usual. It was quiet, reserved, serious. It didn't seem to fit Howard at all, but Zora appreciated the effort.

"I wouldn't be launching the Beast if I did," said Zora.

"I mean the general area," Howard said. "Any idea where to conduct your search?"

"Sort of," she replied. "I've seen him playing in a park at the edge of town. Over near his house. I was there with some friends one time, and he and this other kid hopped an old fence. There's a big forest on the other side."

"And that's where the fire is," Howard said, not asking.

"Yeah," said Zora. "That's where the fire is."

"You patching me in?" Howard asked.

Zora did just that, sending him Beast's camera feed.

"Thanks," Howard said.

It was always the same imagery when Beast first launched. Zora had programmed its flight path for the first few minutes. It buzzed out of her garage, away from the house, and down her street.

She watched the window on her computer screen as it neared the end of the block, being careful to hover over the treetops. Zora had it specifically programmed to nearly skim the leaves. It made for a more dramatic show when she shared the live feed. But it also meant she needed to monitor the Beast's path carefully. A particularly productive spring season could leave her drone tangled in a mess of branches. She had to keep an eye on its path and be ready to adapt when necessary.

Thankfully, the Beast reached the end of the block. It stopped there, now in hover mode. Its controls automatically switched from its pre-planned flight path to manual. It awaited Zora's commands.

She opened up her desk drawer and retrieved a large black gaming controller. After plugging its USB port into the side of her laptop, Zora pressed the enter button at the control's center. The remote hummed to life, a series of tiny lights powering on simultaneously.

"Taking control," Zora said into her headset.

"I'd expect nothing less," said Howard.

Zora watched the window on her monitor carefully. Her eyes narrowed as she moved her manicured thumbs over the controller, adjusting the Beast's direction with one thumb and its altitude with the other. The hulking form made its way over the treetops, its big frame effortlessly carried by its four heavy-duty propellers.

To Zora, maneuvering the Beast was as natural as writing with a pen or eating with a fork. Out of all the members of SWARM, piloting seemed to come the most naturally to Zora. She had logged so many hours with her drone that it was almost like an extension of her.

"Where are you taking us?" asked Howard.

Zora didn't answer. She was away from her desk, turning on the small TV on her dresser. She had to move a plush pink hippo out of the way in order to see the screen.

"Zora?" Howard said in her ear.

"Sorry," she said, changing the channel to a local news source. They were talking about the forest fire. "Hold on."

Zora turned up the volume. From the looks of things, the fire was raging over by the interstate. The highway passed right through the Danbury property.

The news announcer explained that firefighters were putting up their best effort to contain the blaze before it made its way to the park, but it was already spreading in that direction. Acres were affected, but the fire department thought it had time.

As she watched, Zora realized the fire department only seemed interested in the houses outside the park. But that little boy could be anywhere. He could be in that forest right this very moment. And he would have no idea about the danger coming his way.

Zora sat back in her chair, not sure what to do. She could call the authorities and warn them about the possibility of Hobey being in the woods. But would they take her seriously? She was only acting on a hunch, after all. And she didn't want to put anyone in harm's way if she wasn't even sure of the situation. No, this was something she had to handle on her own.

Zora turned away from the TV and checked the navigation signal coming from her drone on a small pop-up window on her computer screen. She was going in the right direction. She pushed forward on her left joystick, bringing the drone to full speed. It would take a few minutes, but she'd get there soon enough.

"I'm headed to the fire," she said into her headset.

CHAPTER 7

TO FIND THE FIRE

Hobey's nap didn't last as long as he would have liked. He woke up cold and a bit confused. It took him a full minute to realize where he was. He wasn't in his warm bed. He was lying in a pile of leaves in the middle of the woods, and his stomach was grumbling.

Hobey army-crawled out of his fort, making sure to stay low so he didn't knock the whole place down. Once he was out, he stood up and stretched. Turns out, sleeping on the ground was a little less comfy than he had hoped.

He surveyed his surroundings and shivered. His body was starting to warm up, but he still felt a chill, despite the warm, dry air in the forest. The fort was colder than he'd thought it would be.

There was only one solution — a fire. People on survivor shows always had a campfire. He didn't need it for food. His peanut butter sandwiches would be great as is. But if he built a fire, it would make his naps better. Or warmer, at least.

The only problem was, like every other element of camping out in the woods, Hobey had no idea how to make a fire.

He took a deep breath. That's when he smelled it. That smoke smell had not gone away. He had no idea what time it was or how long he had been asleep, but if someone was burning leaves, he thought they'd be done by now.

Suddenly, Hobey stood up straight. Of course! Why hadn't he thought of it earlier? He might not know how to make a fire, but whoever was burning leaves already had one going. All he had to do was find a dry branch, one that would make a good torch. Then he'd sneak onto the fire burner's property, light his branch, and sneak back off. He'd bring the torch back to his camp, and presto! One campfire.

Of course there was the matter of playing with fire. Hobey wasn't allowed to do that at home under *any* circumstances. He wasn't allowed to touch the matches or even throw newspaper onto the fire when they had the fireplace going during the winter. But there were no rules here in the wild. Hobey was a man now, out on his own.

He tilted his head back and took a good, deep sniff. After coughing a few times, Hobey decided the smell was coming from straight ahead. He grabbed a dead tree branch from the base of a nearby maple tree and snapped off a few of the lower limbs until it sort of resembled a torch. One of its ends was covered in brown leaves. Surely, they'd catch fire rather easily.

Branch in tow, Hobey headed deeper into the woods. Then he stopped in his tracks. He pulled his sweatshirt's hood up over his head. This was a sneaky mission. He'd almost forgotten to be sneaky.

CHAPTER 8

THE BLUE THING

"There it is," Zora said.

"Whoa," Howard said in her ear. "That's worse than I thought."

On Zora's screen was an image of eight fire trucks parked on an otherwise deserted stretch of the interstate. Clearly it was no casual gathering.

"They must have closed off the road," Zora said. "The highway is never this empty."

"I can see that," said Howard. "Hold on . . . yeah. Yeah, it's closed for two exits in either direction. Or at least that's what the Internet is telling me."

The Beast hung in the sky above the highway. Zora turned it around. She typed in some commands on her computer as she spoke.

"OK, let's make this our starting point," Zora told Howard. "We can branch out from here. I'm setting the Beast on a flight pattern with a rotating camera. Keep your eyes peeled. We're looking for movement, bright color, anything out of place."

"So I've been meaning to ask . . ." said Howard. "This little guy, he's the brother of a friend of yours?"

Zora thought about it. "No," she said finally. "Not really. I mean, I guess I used to be close with his sister, LeAnn. When we were really little. About her brother's age."

"Yeah?"

"Yeah," said Zora. "Now we're just sort of in different worlds. I fell in with a different crowd."

"Oh, that's right," said Howard. "Unlike the rest of us social misfits, you're one of the cool kids."

"Hey!" said Zora. "So my friends are popular, so what?"

"Doesn't matter if they're popular or not," said Howard. "What matters is that they're your friends, right? Shared interests, deep conversations, good laughs."

"What are you trying to say?" Zora said.

"Me?" said Howard, feigning innocence. "Oh, nothing. Why?"

"I think you're —" Zora stopped as something on the screen caught her eye. She paused the feed, freezing the Beast in midair. It hovered obediently, waiting for her next command. With a few shortcut keys on her keyboard, Zora enlarged the image on her screen.

"There!" she said, a bit too loudly, into her headset. "There's something down there. Something blue."

Blue wasn't a color you came across in the woods that often. It was worth investigating.

Zora grabbed her gaming controller and pointed the right joystick forward. At her command, the Beast dove.

* * *

Hobey Hall thought it was a raven at first — or a crow. Was there a difference between the two? There had to be. He just didn't know what it was. But Hobey didn't particularly like either bird, so when he saw the thing dive through the treetops toward him, he wanted nothing to do with it.

He'd been walking through a heavily wooded area for a good fifteen minutes when he came upon the clearing — and the big blue slab of metal in the middle of it. It looked like a giant shingle or something. Its sides were grooved like the potato chips Hobey liked but much larger. It almost looked like something out of a construction site.

When Hobey had gone to investigate, he'd spotted some orange rust at the corners. He'd tilted one end out of the ground and had been disgusted to find a hundred or so little worm thingies underneath. They looked like grubs or maggots. Maybe they were just beetles.

Hobey wasn't into bugs like his sister was. LeAnn had always found them really interesting, even the wasps that lived under the back porch in those creepy clay-looking nests of theirs. But these things were grosser than anything they had in their little backyard.

Even so, the piece of metal was light. Hobey bent down and lifted it up again. It would probably make a better roof for his fort than those two branches. It would probably keep the rain out better too.

He hadn't had any luck finding the fire, although the scent was much stronger here. He was even pretty sure he'd seen some smoke overhead. He could be getting closer, but the blue piece of metal would have to take priority. He would need to drag it home.

That's when he spotted the crow.

As it turned out, it wasn't so much a bird as a remote-controlled plane. And that wasn't quite right either. Hobey had never seen anything like it. It was like a toy helicopter with four blades. It was cool, like an army toy, and had the same coloring as his military Halloween costume from last year.

As the plane-thing came down from the trees, Hobey ran to hide behind a large bush. It didn't seem to care about him, though. It was hovering over the blue piece of metal.

Hobey stood up and began walking a little closer. That's when the light caught his eye. The sun was reflecting off something on the front of the flying toy. It was a lens. This weird, remote-controlled flying saucer had a camera. And that meant it would see him when it turned around.

Running away from home meant not being spotted. Hobey knew that much. It meant staying away from all people, even robotic flying things. Without another thought, he dropped his would-be torch and started running back in the direction of his fort. Or at least, he hoped that was the direction he was headed.

As Hobey sprinted around trees and over stones, one thought kept running through his head: *Who knew running away would mean this much running?*

CHAPTER 9

GIVING CHASE

"Nothing," said Zora. "Man."

"What is that, some scrap metal?" said Howard.

"Looks like it," said Zora. "I'll do a three-sixty spin. See if we've attracted any attention this low to the ground."

Hovering a few feet above the piece of metal, the Beast began to spin in a slow circle.

"Wait," said Howard. "There. Can you zoom back in on that slab of metal?"

"OK," Zora said. "Hold on." She turned the Beast's camera a little, pointing it downward.

"Huh," said Howard.

"What?" said Zora.

"See that bit of ground there, with those mealworms digging through it?"

"Oh . . ." said Zora. "That shouldn't —"

"Exactly," said Howard. "It's been moved — recently. That section used to be covered. The bugs are still frantic.

Like they're busy running away from whatever took off the roof."

"You think he was here?" said Zora.

"Go back to the three-sixty rotation," said Howard. "Slower this time."

Zora did just that. This time, she spotted something. She tapped a key on her keyboard forcefully. "There!"

On her screen was a tree branch propped up against the trunk of another tree. But the leaves didn't match. It looked like the broken limb of a maple tree resting against a pine tree. What's more, she could see bright white spots all along the limb, like some of its branches had been broken off.

"That looks like it was done by a person," she said.

"What? That stick?"

"Yeah, look how it's propped up there," said Zora. "That doesn't just happen."

"I guess . . ." Howard didn't sound convinced. "So head in that direction?"

"Head in that direction," Zora said. She knew it was a long shot, even if she wasn't saying as much. That limb could have gotten there in any number of ways. The wind could have blown it, or someone could have moved it weeks ago. But they needed a direction to search, and if LeAnn's brother had been here, he was way too close to the fire.

* * *

Hobey would have rather kept on running, but the root sticking out from the ground had other ideas. As soon as his toe hit the root, he felt himself shooting forward. He put his hands out in front of him and braced for impact. He hit the ground with a thud and briefly closed his eyes.

When he opened them, Hobey felt strange. He didn't know where he was or what he was doing. He picked up his head, not noticing the rock it had been resting on. He didn't notice the little trickle of red that ran down the side of his face. He felt woozy, and more than that, he felt sleepy.

Hobey crawled over to a nearby bush and the patch of tall green grass that had sprouted behind it. The grass was glowing, caught in a bright beam of sun that had snuck through the thick tree cover above.

The sun felt warm, the grass dry and soft. That's all Hobey wanted right now. He closed his eyes. His small body nearly disappeared in the tall grass. It was a hiding place. It was a sleeping place. It was a resting place.

* * *

The Beast lurched forward. Slow, meticulous.

It passed by the thick root jutting out from the dirt. It did not stop. It passed over the small rock with the tiny pool of red. It did not stop. It passed by the green bed of tall grass. It did not stop.

CHAPTER 10

THE EMPTY FEELING

Zora let out a sigh. It was the kind of frustrated exhalation that didn't require a follow-up question. But Howard spoke anyway.

"What's the matter?" he asked.

"This. How long have we been searching with nothing to show for it?" she said.

"About an hour and a half now if —"

"It was rhetorical, To," she said, using Howard's last name. This was serious. Howard knew this wasn't a time for conversation. "I know exactly how long we've been searching."

"Maybe he's not out here," he said anyway. "We don't have any real evidence."

"Yeah," said Zora. "But what if . . . what if he is?" Her voice was soft, worried. She looked over at her phone. No text from Gabby or either of the Jessicas. That meant no news.

"Is there somewhere else you could swing by?" Howard asked. "Some other place a lost little kid would go? Let's brainstorm. What did you like to do when you were that age?"

"I don't know. Play video games? Watch TV, I guess. Build . . ." Zora stopped. Her eyes lit up. "Did you see that?!?" she yelled without meaning to.

"Ouch," Howard said.

"Sorry," Zora said, "but look!"

She spun the Beast around, lowering it as it rotated. The hulking camo drone moved gracefully, swooping with a natural precision, like a hawk making a dive for its prey.

Zora's eyes were glued to the Beast's video display. Trees. Bushes. Then there, in the center of the screen. Three rocks — boulders, really. Two leaning against each other, with a third on the ground in front of the others, as if it had grown tired and needed a break from centuries of standing. Two branches leaned against the formation like a roof. But that could be a coincidence. A natural occurrence like the maple branch resting against the pine tree.

It was the stick that got Zora's attention.

The thing was about four feet tall. All of its smaller branches had been snapped off, as if someone had been trying to craft it into a spear. Or more accurately, a flagpole. At the top was a tiny blue sweatshirt, hanging there for all the world to see. It was a perfect decoration — or declaration — for a second grader.

Zora didn't have a doubt in her mind. She had found Hobey Hall's hideout.

"O-M-G," said Howard.

Zora didn't even have time to roll her eyes. Her brow was furrowed, her eyes focused. This was it. She lowered the drone to the base of the makeshift shelter and directed the Beast's camera lens inside. She hit a button on her keyboard, and a small, focused beam of light near the lens illuminated the inside of the structure.

Leaves. Dry, ruffled, and crunched leaves. And a backpack. Other than that, the fort was empty.

Zora's heart sank. Her stomach felt as if she hadn't eaten in days. For a second, she thought she might throw up.

"I'm calling the police," Howard said.

Zora didn't react at first. After a moment, she said, "Yeah. Good idea."

"I know what you're thinking, Zora," Howard said. "But this is a good thing. We know he's here in the forest. This is proof. It's a step in the right direction."

Zora didn't say anything. Then finally, "We must have missed something. I was sure he was over by that sheet metal."

"OK," Howard said, "let's retrace our steps. But I'm calling the authorities now."

"Go ahead," said Zora. "But it's not our steps we need to retrace. It's *his*."

CHAPTER 11

THE SUNNY PLACE

It wasn't a straight shot from Hobey's shelter to the piece of blue metal near the fire. The direct route was interrupted by a thick, thorny area where the bushes grew together, almost creating a wall. Good for some of the wildlife, but not so good for a second grader intent on heading to the other side. There was an open path, but it was meandering in nature. But then again, so were little boys.

The Beast followed that path, scanning the ground for any clues. Zora kept the speed slow. She couldn't afford to overlook anything. She couldn't afford to let Hobey down. She owed it to him. More than that, she owed it to LeAnn.

Zora didn't often think about the early years of her childhood. But with this situation with Hobey — with LeAnn — she didn't have much choice.

LeAnn had been like a sister to Zora when they were Hobey's age. There'd barely been a weekend that went by without them finding an excuse for a sleepover. And not the girly kind, either. They hadn't painted nails or talked about boys. Instead they'd spent hours planning their futures. They'd planned to start an invention company. They would come up with the newest innovations, the next generation's smartphone or gaming system. They would be pioneers, changing the world for the better. But then . . . it all came apart.

Zora didn't know exactly how it had happened. Maybe because she was more social than LeAnn. She'd wanted to meet new people, try new things. LeAnn had been happy with their sleepovers and mutual daydream sessions. She'd had no interest in the so-called cool table.

At the time, Zora had wanted that . . . or had thought she did, at least. But if that was truly the case, then why had Zora helped form SWARM? And why act in secret? If Zora wanted such different things in life, then why was LeAnn the one to publicly embrace her interests while Zora kept hers to herself?

Zora looked down at her lap. She had avoided this train of thought for a long time. The Beast stopped in place.

"Hey," said Howard in her ear. "You find something?"

Zora shook her head, bringing herself back to the present. Back to the task at hand.

"No," she said. She pressed forward on the left joystick of her controller. She had to keep moving. She had to find Hobey.

The Beast's camera panned back and forth, back and forth. To a casual observer, the drone probably looked like it was shaking its head. As if it disapproved of what was going on.

To Zora, the head-shaking carried greater weight. It was as if her drone knew her too well. He saw who she had become and wasn't proud of it.

It was a silly notion. The thing couldn't think on its own, after all. It could only answer commands. Zora had told it to scan the area. Commanded it to shake its head. Maybe it was Zora who didn't approve of her current lifestyle.

"You know you still have your light on," Howard said, once again breaking her train of thought.

"Hmm?" said Zora. She checked the toolbar on her screen. Howard was right. She'd left the light on ever since she'd used the Beast to peer into Hobey's little lean-to fort.

She moved her hand to the keyboard and was about to shut it off when a glare on the screen caught her eyes. The Beast's flashlight had reflected off something on the ground. That was strange. The ground was dry now. There wasn't enough moisture for a puddle.

Zora turned the drone around slowly, swiveling its camera and directing it to the ground. Below was a large, flat rock. Zora lowered the Beast. On the rock was a dark brown stain and in the center, a small pool of liquid. It was only about the size of a quarter. But the liquid was red. Red liquid. It was blood.

Zora spun the Beast back up, frantically turning it from side to side. No sign of anything out of the ordinary. No sign of an injured animal. No sign of Hobey.

She panned the camera to the left and noticed a bush and a tall patch of grass. Where the grass met the dirt of the forest floor, a few of the weeds seemed trampled. As if someone stomped on them, pushed them out of place, or . . . maybe crawled through them.

"You seeing this?" Zora said into her headset.

"Oh, I'm seeing it," Howard said. His voice was hushed. There was blood, and that was never a good sign.

The Beast hovered slowly through the air. It dodged a tree, climbed up over the bush, and found its way to the patch of tall grass. It was brighter here. The sun was shining through a break in the foliage. But there was nothing. Just tall weeds. Just overgrowth.

Then she saw it. It was just a shoe sticking out of the grass. But that shoe connected to a leg. That leg connected to a body. And that body belonged to Hobey. He was lying there in the grass. And he wasn't moving.

"Call the police," said Zora. "Call them again."

"On it," said Howard.

"Send them my GPS signal," said Zora. "I'm routing it to you now."

"Got it," said Howard. "It'll just take a minute."

"Make it a short minute," she said. "I can't tell if he's OK."

Zora sat back in her chair. She had found him. She'd found Hobey Hall.

She programmed the Beast to land and then stood up, still looking at her screen. She grabbed her cell phone, pushed her chair in, and sprinted out of her bedroom. There was no time to waste. Zora had a forest fire to get to.

CHAPTER 12

NO MORE BREATH

"Hold it right there, miss," said the police officer.

It took Zora a few seconds to realize he was talking to her. She stopped for the first time since she'd left her house, realizing that she was extremely out of breath.

"Can't let you go any farther," the officer said. He stepped away from his position near the wooden fence that separated Whitman Park and the Danbury property and walked toward Zora.

"Huh?" was all she managed to respond.

"This place is cordoned off," he said.

"But . . ." Zora puffed, "but I need to get in there and —"

Just then, she heard a rustling noise in front of her. Someone was walking through the woods. Zora peered into the forest and saw two large shadows making their way toward her. She stood there as silently as possible for someone panting so hard, not saying anything to the officer at her side.

The shapes drew nearer, coming into focus. They were police officers. Two of them. One was carrying something — a backpack. Upon further examination, they both were carrying something. The smaller of the two was carrying a body.

"Hobey," Zora said, losing her breath even further.

The officers came closer. Their pace was quick, despite the thick growth of the woods. Quick but not in a hurry. And then Zora realized why. The body . . . it moved.

In fact, it was moving quite a bit.

"I don't wanna go home!" Hobey said in a weak voice. He kicked one leg, then the other.

He was protesting, but not to the full extent of his abilities. It was like he wanted the world to know he was angry, even if he truly wasn't. It didn't take a police detective to realize that Hobey Hall was secretly happy to be going home. Running away wasn't quite as glamorous as he had expected.

"All right," said the officer carrying him. "I heard you." When he got to the fence, the officer raised Hobey over it and set him down on his feet.

Zora looked at this blond boy who didn't even recognize her. There was a bit of dried blood at his temple, and he looked like he might have mistaken mud for sunblock, but otherwise, Hobey seemed like a normal seven-year-old. A normal, healthy seven-year-old.

Zora breathed a sigh of relief. She looked at the officer next to her with a blank expression at first. Then she smiled. It felt good to smile like that — genuine, happy, relieved. Hobey might not know it, the rescue team might not know it, and LeAnn might not know it. But Zora did. She and the Beast had saved Hobey.

She was still smiling when she returned home to find her mother waiting for her. Zora had cut school, after all. Her mother was in no mood to smile.

CHAPTER 13

STEPS FORWARD

"Erik," said Gabby. "I said Erik was the one talking about you in health class."

"Oh," said Zora. "OK."

Zora turned her head away from the window to face Gabby. The car was once again stopped in front of Zora's house, but she hadn't even noticed. She was in her head. She was somewhere else.

"So," said Gabby, "I'm gonna see you in like an hour, right?"

"An hour?" said Zora. She honestly had no idea what Gabby was talking about.

"This is the last day," said Gabby. "If you're going to try out for the cheer squad, this is it. Normally, Ms. Woodrue wouldn't even be willing to see you so late in the week, but we're short this year, and since we all know you and can vouch for you and —"

"I can't," said Zora.

Gabby blew a stray hair from in front of her face. "Why not?" she said. "What's your excuse this time? Your mom designing you a walk-in closet and wants to know where to hang the chandelier?"

"Because I don't want to," said Zora.

Gabby furrowed her brow. "That's it?"

Zora shrugged. It was time to start being honest — or at least *more* honest — about what she really wanted. "Sorry, Gab," she said. "You like it, and that's fine. But it's not for me. It's your thing. I mean, you're good at flipping or whatever."

Gabby smiled. She knew she was being insulted, but it was her favorite kind of insult. It was padded with a compliment.

"So, you're just going to sit at home all night?" said Gabby.

"No. Maybe," said Zora. "I don't know. Maybe I'll go see what the girls at the computer lab are up to tonight."

Gabby looked at Zora and made a face. It looked somewhat like a mixture of disgust and confusion. "You like that stuff?" Gabby finally said.

"Yeah," said Zora. "I've always liked that sort of thing."

"Huh," said Gabby. She was quiet for a moment, thinking about something. It was like she had just made the discovery of a lifetime.

Zora braced herself for what was next. *This is it,* she thought. *The moment everything changes.*

"So, you could, like, help me figure out the online PSAT stuff? After cheerleading practice, obviously. I mean, priorities, right?" Gabby said.

Zora smiled. Nope. It was still Gabby. And if Gabby was anything, she was consistent. "Sure," she said, nodding and getting out of the car. "Thanks for the ride."

"Wait!" Gabby called as Zora neared her front door. "Can you edit photos too? I really want to change the background of my profile pic so it looks more dramatic, you know?"

Now Zora was smiling. "Yep," she said. "We'll talk about it tomorrow."

She turned the key in the lock and pulled off her shoes. Then she shut the door and walked slowly up to her room, wondering if Howard was online. Her socks touched the carpet gently. One foot in front of the other. She took small steps today. Baby steps.

CHAPTER 14

THE MAN IN THE DARK CAR

The Man in Black was listening to classical music. It always soothed him on days like today. Los Angeles traffic was never easy, and rush hour was quickly approaching. The roads were far from clear, so the Man in Black enjoyed the private symphony from the cool interior of his vehicle.

His car was black. His suit was black. His sunglasses were as dark black as they came. Even his hair was black, slicked back on his head. It was a stark contrast to his complexion. But the Man in Black liked contrast. He liked his life in black and white, even if he operated in a world full of grays.

The Man in Black smiled a bright white smile. He had perfect teeth. He prided himself on his dental hygiene. He had spent a small fortune on whitening, crowns, and mouth guards over the years, but he had a million-dollar smile to show for it. He used that grin whenever possible. Now he was using it because he'd discovered a parking spot, right there across from the hotel. It couldn't be more perfect.

He required only one attempt to parallel park his jet-black sedan. He stepped out of the car, looking from right to left, then from left to right. A crowd was forming outside the hotel, but no one had noticed him. To them, the Man in Black was nothing special. That was how he preferred things. He wasn't in the market for witnesses, after all.

The Man in Black pressed a button on his keychain, and the trunk of his dark car popped open. He walked to the back of the sedan and removed a single item from its trunk. The thing in his hands was as black as his suit. It was as sleek as his hair. It was fairly small, despite its powerful motor, and had four small blades, one mounted on each corner.

He placed the device on the sidewalk near the car and then got back inside behind the wheel. He shut his door, then reached over and opened the glove box. Inside was a black remote, complete with two joysticks, a few buttons, and a small monitor. He pressed the center button, and the controller vibrated to life in his hands.

Outside the car, the small object began to hum quietly. Then it lifted up into the air, propelled by four rapidly spinning miniature blades. The dark drone rose up into the sky.

The Man in Black sank into his seat. He moved the controls with his long, rough thumbs. He smiled his bright smile, even though no one could see him. This time, the smile wasn't for them. It was for him alone.

CHAPTER 15

SNACK, INTERRUPTED

"I'm going to need you to explain this," Howard To's father said, placing the note on the kitchen table.

Howard took a bite of his cereal, trying his best to avoid making eye contact with his dad. He knew what it was. He'd played hooky from school — again — two weeks ago. He was surprised it had taken so long for his parents to be notified.

"Howard," his dad said. It was one word, but somehow it was also a complete sentence.

"Sorry, Pop," Howard said. "I just . . . couldn't do it."

"You've been missing too much school," said his dad. He sat down in the empty wooden chair next to Howard. "We need to talk about this. If you're being bullied —"

"Dad!" Howard said, mortified even though they were the only two people in the kitchen. "I'm not being bullied. Jeez. I haven't had a bully since, like, the first grade."

Feeling his dad's gaze on him, Howard shifted in his seat. He was uncomfortable in his academy-issued uniform — a navy polo shirt and slacks. Everyone at his private school wore the same thing, but for some reason, Howard appeared more grown up than his peers. He had been told he had "old eyes" — whatever that meant.

"Then what is it?" Dad asked. He scratched the top of his head, his fingers finding their way through his thinning black hair.

That simple act annoyed Howard. But then again, nearly everything his parents did annoyed him in some way. He couldn't explain it.

"It's nothing," Howard said. "I just get bored."

"You'd rather play with that remote-controlled helicopter of yours," said his dad. His eyes narrowed.

"It's called a drone, Dad," said Howard, rolling his eyes. "You know that. You were there when I bought it."

This was Howard's sore spot, and his dad knew it. He brought it up any time he was trying to win a fight. The drone wasn't just a hobby to Howard. It was a way of life.

"And I never would have allowed it if I knew it would get in the way of your studies."

"Get in the way? I have all As. I always have all As," said Howard. He stood up from the table and brought his bowl over to the sink. "School bores me out of my mind. They dumb everything down!"

Howard dumped the remainder of his cereal into the stainless steel sink. He mashed the soggy flakes down into the garbage disposal. Down and out of sight. He didn't bother to turn the disposal on, though.

"You're sixteen," said his dad. "You go to school. Every day. I don't care how above it you think you are. Those are the rules. And when you're an adult, guess what? You'll go to work every day. That's life."

"That's your life," said Howard under his breath.

He didn't dare say it at full volume. He was angry, he was annoyed, but he still respected his father. His dad worked hard to ensure Howard had a place in private school. Howard's family was all about work ethic. His grandfather had worked hard in some dirty factory when he came to California from Vietnam, saving so his father could go to college. Howard's father had inherited that trait, often working holidays and weekends to pay for Howard's schooling. He made sure they had a nice house in the suburbs, a car that matched everyone else's, food on the table, and clothes in the closet.

Howard understood all of that, but he was not his father, and he was most certainly not his grandfather. He wanted something else, something he couldn't quite put into words. But whatever it was, he knew he was tired of waiting for it.

CHAPTER 16

WHIRS AND CLICKS

Angelica Ramone closed her eyes and gently massaged the bridge of her nose with her index finger. She had a headache but had taken her last aspirin a few hours ago. At least the back of the town car was cool and quiet. She could hear the noise outside, but it was muffled, removed. It reminded her of a television set through a shared wall in an apartment building.

Angelica thought back to her Brooklyn apartment from college. She thought about the loud neighbor who would laugh at TV shows so hard his laughter could be heard through the wall. She had been annoyed at first, but when he'd moved out, when his laughter had stopped, she had kind of missed him.

She missed everything about that apartment now. She missed going outside for a jog. She missed walking to the grocery store, even if the trek was uphill. Most of all, she missed sitting in a café with a cup of coffee and a good book.

But Brooklyn was a long time ago. This was Los Angeles. This was her current life, and she couldn't hide in the back of a car for the rest of it. Even if she wasn't ready to open the car door and face what was outside.

Angelica sighed and put on sunglasses with large, dark lenses that nearly covered her entire face. She unlocked the door and stepped out. The sun hit her first, but the camera flashes were a close second. Although why they'd need a flash on a day like today was beyond her.

It was sunnier than usual, and that was saying something. L.A. was always sunny. A few dozen photographers clustered outside her hotel. Ever since her breakup with Bradley Wilt, they'd been out in full force. But Angelica blamed herself for that. This is what she got for dating a co-star.

"Angelica! Over here!" a familiar voice called. It was the paparazzo with the George Lucas beard. Angelica recognized him right away. He was always there.

Next to him stood his friend, the woman who always shouted to her in both English and Spanish. "Angelica!" the photog yelled, followed by a sentence in Spanish.

Angelica didn't understand a word of it. She'd taken French in high school, and she wasn't even good at that language. She wasn't about to look either way, though. Not today. Posing for a photo was the last thing on her mind. She just wanted to get inside, take something for her headache, and collapse on the oversized California king in her suite.

She'd been living at the hotel for two weeks now and had put no real effort into looking for a permanent residence. The hassle with the paparazzi was annoying, but even so, she couldn't bring herself to think about relocating, let alone hire movers.

Despite what the army of photographers thought, Angelica was a person. She wasn't an object. She wasn't a robot who played make believe in hit film after hit film. She had just as many thoughts, opinions, and feelings as anyone else. She would deal with her breakup on her own terms and at her own pace.

As Angelica approached the hotel, the bellhop opened the door, smiling his usual nervous smile. Angelica always found it cute that he was so kind. Every time he was working, he tried his best to accommodate her, despite the nonsense outside.

She patted him on the shoulder as she walked by, breathing in the cold hotel air. In a few seconds, she'd be safe. She'd be alone in her room.

The bellhop hurried behind her as she walked to the elevator. He placed his key in the special slot below the row of buttons, then pressed the special suite button, marked *SU1*.

Angelica leaned her head back against the mirrored wall as the elevator climbed to the very top floor. The doors of the evalator opened, not onto a hallway, but directly into Angelica's room. She handed a folded-up fifty-dollar bill to the bellhop, who promptly rejected it with a wave of his hand.

"No, ma'am," he said. "That's too much. It's an honor enough to —"

"No," Angelica cut him off. "Take it. It's the least I can do."

The bellhop took the bill without looking at it and shoved it into his pocket. He seemed more than a little embarrassed. "Th-thank you," he said, almost under his breath.

Angelica walked into her foyer as the elevator closed behind her. She popped one shoe off, then the other. She was happy to be rid of the high heels. She hadn't even noticed that her feet were hurting until this very moment. In the large bathroom she found her aspirin and took two. Then she walked into her bedroom.

The room was a little cold, so she made her way to the balcony's sliding door and pulled it open. The warm breeze hit her. Angelica took five steps and then collapsed on the bed. Finally, she was alone. She could drop her guard. She could have . . . the thought entered her mind like a bolt of lightning. It was in the freezer! She'd completely forgotten about it.

With a burst of energy, Angelica made a beeline to her suite's living room and adjoining full kitchen. She opened the freezer, and there it was: double-fudge brownie ice cream with that amazing chocolate swirl. Becky had come through again.

Angelica had once cringed at the idea of hiring a personal assistant, but Becky had been a godsend. And acquiring a particularly hard-to-find ice cream seemed to be her specialty.

Pint in one hand, spoon in the other, Angelica made her way back to her bed. She hit the button on the TV remote on the nightstand and popped the ice cream's lid. Then she dug in, shoveling the ice cream to her mouth in enormous spoonfuls.

The TV was loud. Louder than Angelica intended, but she couldn't be bothered to turn it down. She didn't share a wall with anyone these days, and she was exhausted. It was some type of nature show. A wolf was howling at the moon. The sound filled her suite, so loudly that Angelica didn't even notice the whir and clicks from the drone outside her balcony window.

CHAPTER 17

UNDER THE BED

Howard trudged up to his room. He thought about slamming his door, but instead, he simply shut it quietly. Then he knelt beside his bed and pulled out a large, custom control panel. Howard had modified an old video game controller from the 1980s — the kind with a black joystick with a ball on the end — and improved it using spare parts from some of the computer mods he'd been messing with on the weekends.

The end result was a panel about the size of a board game box, with dials and switches, all with a retro look. It was like something from an airplane cockpit in an older movie. Or at least the arcade version of one.

One by one, Howard flipped a series of switches. In the corner of his room, his computer powered on. In another corner, his speakers whined to life. He plugged a black headset into the side of his control panel and heard a familiar voice in his ear.

"About time you joined us, HowTo." It was the perky, always optimistic sound of ParkourSisters. That wasn't Parker Reading's real name, of course, just her screen name. It fit her. A pun within a pun. A tough name for a tough girl. But it was a goofy kind of tough, like her sense of humor.

"It's almost like you — gasp — went to school today!" said another voice. It was feminine as well but more sarcastic. It belonged to Zor_elle — Zora Michaels in real life — the other female member of their online group.

Zora lived in Indiana and was probably Howard's closest friend. No . . . that wasn't quite right. She was the person in the group who shared the most of his interests. Howard was into all things fantasy, from movies starring trolls and elves, to role-playing games featuring wizards and warlocks, to comic books, Zora's main interest.

"I put in my hours," said Howard. "Sai here too?"

"If you'd check your monitor once in a while, you'd know the answer to that question is no," Zora said.

"Hey, I don't mock the beauty salon you call a bedroom, you don't mock my retro gaming style," Howard said.

"I should have never let you Skype with me," Zora said.

"Hold on. You Skype with HowTo?" said Parker. "What about me?"

"I'm never home when you send me a request," said Zora.

"I'm sending you one now," said Parker.

"Oops," said Zora. "Dad's calling. Time for dinner. Talk to you guys tomorrow!"

There was a beeping sound in Howard's ear signaling Zora had disconnected from the chat. It seemed harder and harder to get everyone online at the same time. But that's what happened when your team was spread across the entire country.

Howard To, Parker Reading, Zora Michaels, and Sai Patel had never met in person, but they were more than just Internet friends. Sure, they'd all met on a message board originally, but their friendship had blossomed when they'd discovered a shared interest. They were all drone pilots with their own remote-operated UAVs — Unmanned Aerial Vehicles. With Sai's design expertise to help them, they'd formed their own secret message board. But more than that, they'd formed a community.

They'd decided to call their group SWARM — the Society for Web-Operated Aerial Remote Missions. They would use their love of drones to help other people. They'd take their hobby and do something good with it.

Although they'd had a few bumps in the road getting started, SWARM was now stronger than ever. It was a tight-knit group of four, and Howard had never known a support system quite like it — even if they weren't always working on the same case.

Parker started talking again. "It's because she's a girly girl," she said. "She thinks I'm gonna judge her."

"That's because you *will* judge her," said Howard. Now that they were alone on the line, he felt a bit more at ease. He wasn't sure why.

"Fair point," said Parker. There was laughter in her voice. "So what's up at the To household?"

"Just the usual parental lectures laced with disappointment," said Howard. "What's up in the big city?"

"Oh, you know. New York is still New York. One of the kids at my school fell on the subway tracks," she said. "But I helped pull him out with this other guy."

"Whoa!" said Howard. "That's crazy."

"Not really," said Parker. "There's always someone messing around on the platform. And there wasn't a train in sight."

"So who's this other guy? Your superhero partner?"

"I love this sound," said Parker.

"What?" Howard asked, confused.

"The sound of Howard To getting jealous. It's like my favorite thing in the world."

"I am not jealous," said Howard, rolling his eyes, even though he knew Parker couldn't see him. "Just curious about this guy you're hanging out with."

"Hey, speaking of red-hot love —"

"Wait, what red-hot —"

"Your girlfriend made the news today," Parker said.

"My girlfriend?"

"Angelica Ramone."

"Ooooh . . ." said Howard, finally getting the joke. *"That* girlfriend."

"You have so many," Parker quipped. "It must be hard to keep track."

"It's a curse, really," said Howard, smiling. "So what about Angelica? What happened?"

"Check your screen," Parker said. "It looks like she's not taking her recent breakup very well."

Howard stood up, tucking his control panel under one arm. He walked over to his desk to look at his state-of-the-art flat-screen computer monitor. On the screen, a pop-up window waited for him. Using the track pad on his control panel, Howard clicked on it and opened an instant message window with ParkourSisters.

There, in the attached photo, was Angelica Ramone, looking as amazing as ever. Beautiful big eyes, her trademark full bottom lip, blond hair falling to her shoulders. She was sitting on a white comforter in an expensive-looking hotel room and furiously eating a pint of chocolate ice cream.

At first Howard smiled, appreciating this rare glimpse into Angelica's private life. He usually wasn't big on celebrities, but there was something special about Angelica. He'd had a crush on her for the better part of a decade. He'd even felt a strange rush of hope when he heard she'd broken up with her longtime boyfriend. Every time he traveled into L.A. from his suburb, he hoped he'd see her walking down the street or into some fancy restaurant. But he never had any luck.

"Huh," Howard said into his headset. "How did they . . . this isn't from a photo shoot."

"What do you mean?" asked Parker.

"This looks like it was taken at that fancy hotel, the Carmichael. She's staying there," he said.

"Um, stalk much?"

"Seriously," Howard said, "how did the paparazzi get this shot?"

For a long moment Parker didn't say anything. "You don't think . . ." she finally spoke.

"Yeah," said Howard. "I do."

"Bird in the air?"

"Already on it," said Howard.

He pressed a button on his control panel. It was red, the most noticeable button on the device. There was even text meticulously printed on the button. In capital letters, it read *LAUNCH*.

CHAPTER 18

OUT OF THE DOGHOUSE

There was a doghouse behind Howard To's house. The strange thing was, the To family had never owned a dog. The structure had come with the house when they'd bought it nearly ten years ago. The previous owners had managed to take the swing set with them — a heavy blow to six-year-old Howard at the time — but had left the doghouse in all its faded green glory.

It was a lone structure in an overgrown backyard that had taken the To family three years to get in order. No one gave it much thought aside from Howard. When he was little, he'd been able to fit inside. It had served as his playhouse of sorts. By third grade, it had become his soccer goal. Its small opening had been a challenging target. And now, the doghouse served its greatest purpose yet. It was home to Howard's "pet." It was the launching pad for his drone.

When Howard pressed the *LAUNCH* button on his control panel, the drone came to life. The dust and dirt on the ground scattered to the doghouse's interior walls, like they were rushing to take cover from unexpected danger. In the center of the house, resting in its charger base, the red drone's four black blades spun feverishly.

Soon the whirring rotors created enough lift to raise the craft off its base. It moved forward, following a carefully plotted course Howard had programmed more than a year ago. The shiny red plastic glistened in the California sun as it escaped the shade of the doghouse. As the machine rose into the air, the red-and-yellow flame decals on each side of the main body became apparent.

The drone, which Howard had named the Redbird, was in no way a modest aircraft. It was the race car of SWARM and the boldest side of Howard's personality. Sure, it was efficient with its small camera and sleek design. But it wanted the world to know it was there. It hummed almost silently in flight, but visually, it was as loud as drones came.

"Redbird is up," said Howard into his headset.

"Can you patch me in?" said Parker.

"Yes, ma'am," said Howard, pushing a few buttons on his control panel.

"Nope," Parker replied.

"What, the feed isn't working?" Howard asked. "I can see it on my end."

"Nope to the ma'am talk," said Parker. "I'm like a half year younger than you."

Howard smiled. "Gotcha, Grandma," he said.

"You can't tell, but I'm kicking you over the Internet," said Parker.

Howard didn't answer. He was too busy typing something into the keyboard section of his control panel. Then finally, he said, "OK. I'm setting a course to the Carmichael now."

"Look at you, out to play white knight to your damsel in distress," said Parker.

"Now who's jealous?" Howard said.

"I don't know," Parker replied. "Is that a trick question?"

CHAPTER 19

CRASHING DOWN

"Of course I didn't plan it, Jacob," Angelica Ramone snapped at the man across the table from her. He didn't seem to be paying attention to her, despite her serious tone.

"OK, then walk me through it," Jacob replied. He was shorter than Angelica, but sitting at the rooftop café, they looked equal in height.

"There's nothing to walk through," Angelica said. "Someone invaded my personal space. They took a picture of me inside my hotel room."

"So they were out on your balcony?" Jacob said. He took a sip from his coffee cup. Part of the creamy drink stuck to his upper lip, giving him a makeshift mustache. He wiped it with a napkin, much to Angelica's relief.

"I don't know," Angelica said. "I don't know how they'd get up to the top floor. The Carmichael is the tallest building in that section of town."

"So we're talking about a telescopic lens from a nearby building?"

"I said I don't know," Angelica said, sounding more agitated now. "All I know is that it's an invasion of my privacy. I was on my bed."

"I know, I saw the photo."

"*Everyone* saw the photo. Didn't you read the papers? 'Depressed Angelica Eats Away Her Sorrows' — the tabloids had a field day with it."

"I don't know what you want me to do here," Jacob replied, shaking his head.

"You're my lawyer, Jacob," she said. "Just . . . just do *something.*"

Jacob didn't respond. The photo was out there. There was nothing they could do at this point. Anything posted on the Internet was permanent. There was no getting around it, especially for a celebrity like Angelica.

Angelica sipped her coffee while Jacob thought things through. At least they were alone on the rooftop. Sure, there were paparazzi outside. They'd started gathering as soon as word spread that she was meeting her lawyer here for coffee. But this rooftop seating was reserved for Hollywood's A-list. Which was probably why Angelica liked it so much. No one would bother her up here.

Angelica's thoughts drifted to her ex, Bradley. And then to Sammy, the German shepherd puppy he'd adopted a month ago. If she was honest with herself, she missed the dog more than the boyfriend. At least Sammy had been a good listener.

It hit her all at once. The heartbreak. The never-ending public scrutiny. Sammy. It all seemed to come crashing down on her. Before she even realized what she was doing, Angelica had her face in her hands, crying.

The whole thing seemed to take Jacob by surprise. He didn't know exactly what to do. He certainly didn't know what to say. He just froze in place. He looked like a statue.

Angelica took off her sunglasses. She wiped her eyes with her fingers. "Do you have a tissue?" she asked. She was instantly embarrassed by how weak her voice sounded.

"Oh, yes, yes," said Jacob. He popped open his briefcase, reached inside, and pulled out a pack of tissues. He might not be much use in an emergency, but at least he came prepared for one.

Angelica took a tissue and blew into it. She almost looked like a cartoon character blowing into a cloth handkerchief. Then she looked up, and Jacob cringed despite himself.

"What?" she said.

He reached into his briefcase and handed her another tissue. "You got a little . . ." He trailed off, not wanting to finish his own sentence.

Angelica covered her face. Her cheeks turned a shade of bright red. She snatched the tissue from Jacob and wiped the disgusting display from under her nose. She couldn't remember the last time she had felt this embarrassed. Wait, yes she could. It was when that unflattering picture of her eating ice cream in bed had surfaced on the Internet the night before. At least no one besides Jacob was here to see her . . .

Click.

This time Angelica heard it. It was quiet up on the café's rooftop. There was no loud television to drown out the sound.

She looked up from the table to see a black drone with a camera lens in its center hovering in the air. The lens was focusing on her, clicking rapidly now.

Angelica's mouth fell open. The drone had seen everything. Her blowing her nose like a child. Her crying like a schoolgirl dumped by her prom date. All her raw, private emotions captured for everyone to see. This was how they'd caught her in her hotel room. It was all the fault of this evil jet-black machine.

Jacob was blissfully unaware of the whole situation. He had no idea why Angelica started shouting. He didn't know why she stood up and quickly positioned her dark sunglasses over her eyes. And he didn't understand why she stormed off the rooftop, down the stairs to the café, and out onto the street below.

"Miss Ramone!" a man shouted from the sidewalk. He was right next to Angelica, but he was shouting anyway.

"Angelica!" said another man. "How does it feel to be single again?"

Angelica didn't answer. The crowd outside the café flashed their cameras and screamed their questions. They followed her as she made her way to her car and kept pace with her as she backed out of her parking space, nearly hitting the woman with the too-large camera. And they even jogged after her as she drove away.

CHAPTER 20

THE FIRST MEETING

"There!" Howard shouted into his headset.

"Come on, man," said Parker. "You trying to deafen me?"

"Look," said Howard, pointing at his computer monitor in his bedroom. It took him a second to realize that Parker couldn't see him. She was on the other side of the country, in New York City. Even though it felt like it at times, she was certainly not in the room with him.

"What am I looking at?" Parker said.

"I saw another drone fleeing the scene," said Howard. "How could you miss it?"

"Do you want the honest answer?" Parker asked. Her voice was playful as usual. "I've been watching kung fu movies this whole time we've been talking."

"Hold on!" said Howard. He, on the other hand, was quite serious at the moment. He was working the controls on his large panel with total focus. This was intense, and it required all Howard's concentration.

"Honestly, your whole celebrity crush thing is a little boring," Parker continued, knowing she'd be ignored. She was having fun with him now. She always had fun ruffling Howard's feathers.

Howard didn't answer. He was busy piloting. The other drone was in his sights again. While he couldn't make out all the details, it was clear the thing was expensive. It had a large camera that Howard could even see from the back.

The Redbird swooped downward at the restaurant. Then it buzzed the same rooftop as its prey and dove over the same awning. The other drone was moving a bit slower than the Redbird, and Howard thought he'd be able to catch up to it in another second or two.

"So . . . what's the endgame here?" asked Parker. "You going to try to knock that thing out of the sky? I'm no lawyer, but that's gotta be illegal."

"He's the one . . ." Howard said, trailing off as he forced the Redbird into another dive with the thrust of his joystick. "He's the one breaking the law."

"He was just flying over that restaurant," said Parker. "Who's he hurting?"

"He took pictures of Angelica in her hotel room!" Howard said. "That's not right!" He had almost caught up to the black drone now. And better yet, it didn't seem to have noticed him.

"So you can prove that?" said Parker. "You know for sure that this is the same drone?"

"Well, no, but —" Howard started.

Just then, the black drone spun around and came to an abrupt stop in midair. The Redbird had been spotted.

"Watch out!" screamed Parker in Howard's ears. Now she was the one yelling.

Howard jolted back in his chair and yanked his left joystick up. "Eeeayyyhhh!" That was as close as he could get to an actual word.

The Redbird immediately obeyed his commands. It climbed up sharply, avoiding the hovering black drone by mere inches.

Howard regained his composure, as did the Redbird. He slowed his speed and circled it back around until he was facing the black drone again — or at least he thought he was. But the other drone had disappeared.

"Where is it?" Parker was saying.

"I-I thought it was right there!" said Howard. "How long did it take me to turn around?"

"Long enough, I guess," said Parker.

Howard pointed the Redbird at the ground. There was an alley below, but no one in it. He took the Redbird in a large circle, searching for any signs of movement.

"Is that it?" Parker said. Something dark had just ducked over the neighboring building, and her voice was filled with excitement.

"Going to top speed," Howard said. He positioned his fingers on his control panel to do just that.

The Redbird buzzed forward. The flames on its sides seemed appropriate as it swerved around a billboard and turned a corner. Perched there on the rooftop's ledge was the moving thing Parker had noticed on her screen. But now it was still. It seemed almost afraid. At the very least it was concerned, on edge.

It was not, however, the black drone. It was a pigeon.

"Yeah . . . so that's not the drone," said Parker.

"You think?" said Howard, his tone a little more annoyed than hers.

"I think you lost him," she said.

"*I* lost him, huh?" Howard said. There was more kindness in his voice now. Parker had a way of making him smile, even in the most frustrating of circumstances.

"You only have yourself to blame," she said in her familiar sarcastic tone.

"I'm gonna do another sweep of the area before I head back home to recharge," Howard said.

"I'm gonna rewind my kung fu movie and see what parts I missed," said Parker.

"You do that," Howard said. He smiled, but he made sure he didn't laugh. Parker didn't need any more encouragement.

* * *

The few paparazzi who remained outside the café after Angelica's departure didn't pay any attention to the Man in Black across the street. They were too busy making calls and trying to find out the next hot location to push their cameras into someone's face.

If any of them had glanced at the Man in Black, perhaps they would have noticed his face. Perhaps they would have wondered what could have made this odd gentleman smile. No one had gotten a photo of any importance. No one had taken a shot that would pay a significant amount of money or make the front cover of a magazine.

But there he was, smiling.

The Man in Black picked up his black drone from the sidewalk and placed it in his trunk. Then he got inside his dark car and drove away.

CHAPTER 21

CAUGHT IN THE ACT

"Really, Mr. To?" said Dr. Fletcher as he took the cell phone out of Howard's hands.

Howard didn't respond. He'd been too engrossed in the story he was reading and had forgotten to mind his surroundings. Dr. Fletcher had stopped talking a few seconds ago. That should have been the first clue.

The teacher had been droning on and on about hydrogen molecules, as if Howard really needed a refresher course in a subject he'd studied three years ago. It had seemed the perfect time for Howard to check his email on his phone.

Sure, phones were strictly prohibited in class, but Howard had propped his textbook at just the right angle. He'd been sure Dr. Fletcher couldn't tell what he was doing. So he'd clicked the link Parker had emailed to him.

In retrospect, Howard probably hadn't given Dr. Fletcher enough credit. Perhaps he was a bit sharper than some of the other teachers. He did have a doctorate, after all. Maybe he'd taken a course on how to spot slackers — or maybe Howard just wasn't as clever as he thought he was.

"Let's see here," said Dr. Fletcher, inspecting the smartphone in his hand. "Looks like Howard's got himself a crush — Angelica Ramone." The class began to snicker and giggle. "Well, I can't say you have bad taste."

The teacher walked up to the front of the class and put Howard's phone in his desk drawer. "You can have that back at the end of the day," said Dr. Fletcher. "It'll come wrapped in a shiny new letter for your parents to sign."

That was the last thing Howard needed, but at least he was *at* school today. His parents couldn't get mad at him for skipping again.

Every day in this bland, boring building seemed like a waste to Howard. High school was not his thing. He had a few friends, sure, but *few* was the operative word. He really hadn't met anyone he clicked with outside of Drone Academy.

Howard smiled, despite his current situation. Drone Academy — Parker had made up that name. As if SWARM wasn't enough of a title. She had to add her spin to it. Her color commentary always made his day.

To be fair, Parker's nickname was somewhat accurate. SWARM *was* a school of sorts. Howard wouldn't be half the pilot he was today without Parker's tips, or Zora's, or even Sai's. They all helped each other out in their various missions, and Howard learned something every time.

And although he wasn't even sure what the Angelica mission *was*, Parker was his partner on it. Whether he liked it or not. She'd had a point yesterday. If Howard was going to take down that black drone, he had to catch it doing something illegal.

Before his phone had been confiscated, Howard had had enough time to scan the article Parker had sent. It showed the most unflattering photos of Angelica that Howard had ever seen. She was crying at that café, covered in tears and snot and smeared makeup. It was a far different view than what the media normally showed. Angelica was usually so poised and perfect.

Seeing her human like that didn't lessen Howard's crush on her, however. It just made him want to help her even more.

He opened up his notebook and began to scribble down ideas for drone modifications. He'd been brainstorming since last night and figured he might as well draw up a rough sketch now. If he was lucky, he might even be able to start construction during study hall. He had some of the raw materials in his locker, and it wouldn't take too long.

Howard started drawing faster, looking up occasionally to make sure Dr. Fletcher wasn't watching. So far, so good.

Seventeen minutes later, the bell rang. Howard again looked up at Dr. Fletcher. The teacher was indeed watching Howard now, shaking his head.

Howard stacked his chemistry book on top of his notebook and made his way to the door. He felt lighter without his phone, which wasn't a good feeling. Howard was scrawny enough. Being lighter wasn't a good thing.

* * *

The elevator came to a smooth stop on the fifty-fifth floor. Angelica secured the scarf around her hair. The L.A. sun was brilliant as she stepped out onto the rooftop, even through the dark shade of her sunglasses.

Two men — a large man wearing dark sunglasses and a small man wearing regular eyeglasses — escorted her across the roof. The small man said something into his walkie-talkie as he trailed behind. Angelica couldn't quite make it out. The tall man was walking her forward, like she was the president. Like the safety of the country depended on Angelica making it across that rooftop.

Normally, Angelica found this sort of heightened security annoying. She always appreciated the work of bodyguards, but she hated restrictions to her freedom. But today, with the fresh memory of that black drone spying on her, she didn't mind the escort at all.

Less than a minute later, Angelica found herself being helped up into a helicopter. The chopper had the hotel's logo emblazoned across its side. It was almost enough to make her transfer hotels. The Carmichael was nice, but the private helipad at this particular establishment was certainly enticing.

The door of the helicopter closed, leaving Angelica alone with the pilot. The pilot, a young woman, turned around to smile at Angelica. She was younger than Angelica had expected. But there was a confidence in her eyes that said she knew what she was doing — or she was really good at faking it.

Either way, Angelica didn't feel a rush of adrenaline or fear when the helicopter rose off the fifty-fifth floor of the hotel. She looked out the window. No black drone in sight. No, as they took off, Angelica felt nothing but relief.

CHAPTER 22

TAKING THE SHOT

"He's here somewhere," Howard was saying to Parker.

"And you're sure?" Parker asked through the headset. "Maybe this guy was just a fan and decided he had enough. He might even be a bigger fan than you are . . ."

Howard didn't appreciate the tone. Parker was kidding, but she seemed more serious than usual. She wasn't being playful about it.

"Listen," he said, "if I could find out her location just by checking a hotel employee's Facebook page, so could the other guy."

"The black knight," said Parker. "Good thing a noble white knight is here to save the lady's honor."

"Boy, you're fun today," said Howard. He didn't know what he'd done to make her mad, but Parker didn't seem in the mood for their mission. She seemed to disapprove of it entirely.

"I do what I can," said Parker. And with that, her tone was light again. She seemed back to her old self.

Howard didn't have time to think about Parker's sudden change in attitude. He was on the hunt for the black drone.

"All right, there's the helicopter," he said. "And it's lifting off now . . ."

Howard had positioned the Redbird on the rooftop of the hotel's stairwell and was using its camera to scan the area. Despite the drone's bright coloring, he hoped it wouldn't be spotted. The last thing he wanted to do was make Angelica feel even more threatened. But so far, neither the security team nor Angelica seemed to have noticed Redbird. Howard could only hope the black drone wouldn't notice him either.

"Where are you?" Howard muttered under his breath.

"I'm sitting in my room downing an entire box of cheese crackers," came Parker's response. It wasn't the answer Howard was looking for, but it did make him smirk.

Then he spotted it. As the helicopter lifted off, the black drone rose into view from the side of the building. It began to follow the chopper.

"There it is," he said. "But what is he doing? No way he can keep up with her."

"No way you can, either," Parker said. "What's the plan again?"

"Watch and learn, grasshopper," said Howard.

"Wait, have you been secretly paying attention to my kung fu movie recommendations?" asked Parker.

"Wouldn't you like to know," Howard quipped. "Now, I just gotta get close enough . . ."

The Redbird lifted off its perch and made a beeline for the black drone. With his control panel on his lap, Howard lifted a tiny new remote control from his pocket. It had a single black button in its center. He held the remote tightly in his right hand, steering the Redbird with his left, and studied his computer monitor. He steered the Redbird so that the black drone was framed directly in the center of his live feed.

But the black drone was quicker than the Redbird. Howard couldn't close the distance in front of him.

"I'm gonna have to take the shot," he said.

"What shot?" Parker asked.

Howard didn't answer. He'd spent all of study hall and an hour after school on the Redbird's modifications. His drone was now armed.

A suction-cup pistol, which Howard had owned for nearly a decade, was attached to the side of the Redbird. The gun was small, compact, and could only fire once without a manual reload, but it would have to do. Howard had also added a counterweight on the opposite side of the drone to balance it out and stabilize the vehicle. Then he'd modified the power directed to the Redbird's blades. They needed to spin faster than ever before.

But most of Howard's time that afternoon had been spent on the suction-cup projectile. His toy gun no longer shot its tiny red suction cup bullet — now it shot a tracking device.

It was really a GPS chip, a simple piece of technology easily purchased at an electronics store. Howard had bought his a while ago. He was always buying bits of tech here and there to tinker with. But it wasn't until today that he'd sprayed the chip with a fast-working epoxy. Now, if the GPS chip touched anything, it would adhere to it tighter than a magnet to a refrigerator.

All Howard had to do was fire his gun with the trigger he'd rigged up. That, and not miss.

That was the theory, at least. Howard hadn't had time to test it out.

"Target locked," Howard said, even though he didn't possess the kind of technology needed to lock onto anything. It was just something they said in the movies. He had the black drone in his sights.

Howard pressed the flat button on the remote in his right hand, squeezing it much tighter than necessary. "And . . . firing," he said.

With a rather anticlimactic click, the toy gun shot off. The GPS chip, on its plastic rubber base, shot out of the barrel and sped through the air.

Years of practice with the suction-cup gun paid off. Howard hit his target in one shot — and better yet, it stuck.

The black drone was now flying with a GPS chip attached to its rear.

"Whoa!" said Parker. "You got it!"

"Uh-huh," Howard said, trying to sound confident. He hadn't felt that way, but he didn't want Parker to know that.

"Is that a —" Parker started to say.

"A GPS chip," Howard finished. "I've got his location now. Wherever he goes. I've got him."

Howard slowed the Redbird as the black drone peeled away through the sky. If he hadn't made that shot, there was no way Howard could have kept up. Whoever was piloting that drone had money and tech know-how. But now Howard had time. He could regroup and catch the black drone in the act.

"Way to go, white knight," Parker said in his ear. "You're on your way to a celebrity girlfriend after all."

She was trying to hide it, but her tone had shifted again. Howard wondered why.

CHAPTER 23

HIDE AND SEEK

Angelica looked over the railing of the bridge at her reflection below. It was hazy, just a shadow of her form rippling along with the water of the creek. She smiled. It was the first time she'd been out of focus for a while. It was nice. This trip had been a good idea after all.

The ranch was only a forty-five-minute helicopter ride from downtown Los Angeles. It wouldn't have taken that much longer by car, but Angelica couldn't risk the paparazzi following her. If the tabloids got wind of her visiting her old boyfriend, Jonathan Keaton, she'd never hear the end of it. They were just friends now, but that wouldn't matter. There'd be endless gossip articles about rekindled flames. There'd be jokes on late-night talk shows. And worse, there would be even *more* photographers camped outside her hotel in the morning.

The simple truth was, Angelica needed someone to talk to. Jonathan had always been there for her. Right after the news broke of her split with Bradley, Jonathan had called to offer a friendly ear or a shoulder to cry on. There was nothing romantic about it. When she really thought about it, she realized that Jonathan was her best friend.

"Dinner is almost ready," Jonathan said as he walked out onto the small wooden bridge with her. He was wearing his cowboy hat. Angelica had only seen him wear it on the ranch. "Hope you like your steak well done."

"Not really," she said, smiling at the welcome company.

"Well, too bad," he said. "I overcooked 'em."

"Yet again."

"One of these days I'll pay attention when I've got meat on the grill," he said. "But the Lakers game was on. It was out of my hands."

Angelica put her arm through Jonathan's as he walked her down the path and onto his well-manicured lawn. and leaned her head on his shoulder. This man was like a brother to her. He was family. But yet, the paparazzi would see it another way. She had to hide their friendship for the sake of her own sanity.

"I want to thank you again for —" Angelica stopped talking as soon as she heard it. It was that familiar *whir* and *click*. Just like on the rooftop café. They had found her again. *It* had found her.

Angelica spun around to see the black drone above her. It was hovering in the air, staring at her with its one glass eye. The clicking was rapid now. It didn't want to miss any of what surely was Angelica's new "love affair."

When Jonathan noticed Angelica had turned, he did the same. He looked up at the drone, feeling Angelica release his arm. "What is that . . . wait, is that a drone?"

"It's been following me all week," Angelica said, turning away and covering her face with her hands in a sudden burst of panic. "We need to get inside — now!"

"Wait," said Jonathan. "What about that?"

Angelica turned to look in the direction her friend was pointing. "What?" she said.

"Now there's two of 'em," Jonathan said.

CHAPTER 24

THE END OF THE
WAITING PERIOD

"I can't believe this GPS tracker cost you thirty bucks," Parker said through the headset.

"Thirty-three ninety-nine, to be exact," said Howard. "Worth every penny."

He was busy concentrating on piloting, but there was always time for a little banter. He and Parker had been following the GPS signal for the better part of an hour. Only now did the black drone seem to be slowing down.

"Any idea where you are?" Parker asked in his ear.

"Some sort of ranch," said Howard. "Probably belongs to one of Angelica's friends or something."

"I can see the UAV on screen," said Parker as Howard's drone drew closer to the GPS signal. The black drone was right where the tracker had said it would be.

"Uh-huh," said Howard.

"So now we just observe," said Parker. "Right? We sit and wait and catch it in the act?"

"Uh-huh," Howard said again.

"I only ask because you seem to be picking up speed."

"Uh-huh."

"Howard!" said Parker. Her voice was excited now. "This is totally not the plan!"

"No," said Howard. He pulled back on the joystick on his control panel as hard as he could, picking up even more speed. He was surprised it didn't snap off. "No, it is not."

"Ooooh no," said Parker, almost under her breath.

Howard didn't reply. He had officially run out of patience.

Everything in his life was a waiting game. High school. He had to wait out the boring classes until he could finally challenge himself in college.

Money. He couldn't afford the type of equipment the black drone's owner indulged in. Howard was just in high school, after all. He was usually broke and wouldn't have that kind of income for a decade or so, after he landed a real job.

Girls. He had to wait that out too. Wait for them to notice him. Wait for his youthful quirks to mature into interesting qualities. He'd never had a real connection with any girl he could think of. But while he wouldn't admit it, Howard had a tendency to miss the obvious.

Angelica was different, though. She seemed down to earth. She seemed secure in who she was, not someone looking for attention at every moment. And now Angelica was being stalked, and all he could do was just wait it out. But no, there was one other option.

So that day, as Angelica and her friend hurried to get out of sight, Howard decided to stop waiting. He pointed the Redbird straight toward the unsuspecting black drone. Before Parker could stop him or he could second-guess himself, Howard rammed his drone straight into the other one.

It felt good. When both drones came crashing down to the grass below, Howard felt satisfied.

That is, until Parker spoke.

"Well, that was certainly something," she said.

Howard was smiling when he answered. "That will end that," he said. But his grin only lasted another fifteen seconds. Because after that, the black drone began to move again.

Howard could see it clearly in his camera. The black drone's front blades moved first. It was just a twitch or two initially, but soon they were spinning at top speed, as were the back two blades. Before Howard could let out a word, the black drone was in the air again.

The same couldn't be said for the Redbird. It was completely dead. The collision had totaled three of its four blades, according to the readout on Howard's monitor.

All he could do was sit in his chair and watch the black drone follow Angelica and her friend. It trailed behind them until they were all out of view.

Howard tried to adjust his camera angle, but the camera wasn't working, either. "That couldn't have gone worse," he finally said.

"Oh," said Parker into his ear. "Sure it could've."

CHAPTER 25

NOTES FROM THE RIDE-ALONG

Howard couldn't stop staring at his computer screen. He was speechless. It had been a week since he and Parker had spoken. He had taken some time away from SWARM. Time to mourn the loss of the Redbird and to plan out his next steps.

But even now, a week later, he couldn't find the right words to say. All he could come up with was, "Are you serious? Are you even serious right now?"

"Those two questions are the same question," said Parker. Her voice was lighthearted, but her trademark sarcasm was still there.

"How did you even . . . when did you think to do this?"

"I wasn't the pilot," said Parker. "I was just the ride-along. While you were busy playing drone chicken, I was clicking away. I submitted the pictures as an anonymous tip."

"I just . . . can't get over this," Howard said.

On Howard's screen was a newspaper article — not from a gossip magazine but from a legitimate L.A. paper. The headline read, "Drone Pilot Arrested on Trespassing Charges." On the cover of the paper was a man dressed in black and white. He had black glasses and flawless, slicked-back hair.

"So you took pictures," Howard said. "The whole time I was piloting the drone, you were snapping photos."

"Yep," said Parker. "Well, screen shots. The Redbird was doing all the filming. I was just capturing everything for posterity."

"And you sent them to the press? Shots of the black drone invading Angelica's privacy? Shots of the Redbird fight?"

"All of it," Parker replied. "With a lengthy explanation. I even sent them your address, just in case Angelica Ramone wants to send you back your totaled drone."

"Wow," said Howard.

"Right?" said Parker. "Am I awesome or what? I wouldn't even be surprised if Angelica calls you up some time to personally reward you. You might get that dream date after all."

"About that . . ." Howard said, taking a deep breath. "I think I was kind of . . . I mean, I thought about all the stuff you said this week . . ."

Parker was uncharacteristically silent.

"You were right," said Howard. "I *was* trying to help . . . but it was probably for the wrong reasons. I wanted to be some hero more than I wanted to stop the bad guy. Kinda messed up, huh?"

"Well," said Parker. "Yeah. That's a little messed up. But I'll let it slide. You're a teenage guy, and she's a movie star. It's all good."

"Yeah?"

"Yeah."

"Well, thanks," Howard said. He paused, thinking for a moment how much Parker seemed to get him, then changed the subject. "So I've been meaning to tell you, I got a job this week while I was taking some time off from SWARM."

"Oh, yeah?"

"It's at this local tech startup. No big deal or anything, but I get to fiddle with all sorts of stuff that's above my pay grade."

"Like paper and glue?"

"Ha!" Howard laughed. "Yeah, just like that. But either way, I'll finally have something to keep me busy, you know? Challenge me a little bit."

"Sounds like you can finally save up some money and visit me here in New York," Parker said.

Howard was grinning without realizing it. Blushing a little too.

"Now why would I do that?" he asked.

"Someone needs to rescue me from another summer locked in my poorly air-conditioned room listening to the neighbors argue."

"I can do that," said Howard.

"Of course you can," said Parker. "You're my white knight."

"Takes one to know one," Howard said.

With that, Parker clicked out of the conversation, leaving Howard alone in his room. He stood up, stretched, and walked out through his door. It was time for dinner, and he saw no reason to wait until he was called.

* * *

The Man in Black didn't like the music in the elevator. It was instrumental, like his beloved classical music, but it was modern. Some eighties song he couldn't quite put his finger on. All he knew was that it was awful. It wasn't soothing in the slightest.

When the doors opened, the large police officer ushered him out into the hall. The Man in Black walked through the precinct. No eyes were on him. That didn't bother him at first. It was his job to put the public's eyes on someone else. The more they looked, the more money he made.

Everyone else in the precinct was standing near the corner. It struck the Man in Black as odd . . . until he saw the person they were gathered around.

It was Angelica Ramone, the woman who had made him a lot of money these past few days. Until now. Until she decided to press charges, and the police decided to take his drone. Now she was costing him money.

Angelica seemed to be telling some story to the officers. She was entertaining them, and they were obviously smitten with her. But when the Man in Black was paraded past her, Angelica paused. She locked eyes with the Man in Black. And then she smiled before going back to her story.

The Man in Black did not return the grin. He didn't part his lips and show off his immaculate white teeth. Instead, he looked at the ground. Unlike Angelica, he had no reason to smile.

CHAPTER 26

FOX IN BOX

Chris Fox wasn't after the money. He knew that was how you got caught. When you saw bank robbers in the movies or on the news, they were always going after the teller's drawer.

"Put the money in the bag!" they'd yell as a shocked bank employee filled their gym bag with a few wads of twenties or hundreds. "And no money off the bottom!"

The last bill in each drawer was supposedly marked so the police could find you. Or it activated a hidden alarm. In some cases, a bundle of bills would contain a dye pack that would turn the robber and the money blue as soon as the stolen loot was opened. It all depended on the story the movie wanted to tell.

Chris wasn't sure if any of that was true, but he was not going to risk it. When Chris Fox robbed banks, he avoided the tellers altogether.

That was why, as he walked to the USofA Bank branch on the corner of 5th Avenue and Union Street, it was silent.

This section of Brooklyn was dead at this time of night, so no one had noticed when he'd pulled the ski mask over his bald head and dark goatee. It was cold out, and while it was rare, Chris had seen people wearing this kind of thing in the neighborhood before. Worst-case scenario, someone would assume he was a suspicious guy fighting against Brooklyn's icy winter winds.

"You there yet?" asked a voice in Chris's ear.

It was a familiar sound, one Chris had been hearing nearly his entire life. It was Erich, his younger brother, speaking to Chris through the earpiece he wore in his left ear.

"Hold on, hold on," said Chris under his breath.

"I still think you're nuts, hitting a place this close to your home," said Erich.

"You'll see," Chris whispered in response.

This wasn't the first time Chris's brother had doubted his intelligence. Sure, Erich was the smart one in the family, at least when it came to electronics and computers. But while Erich had spent his life locked away in his room, fiddling with motherboards and computer chips, Chris had been learning how the world really worked. When Chris was sure of a robbery, it meant they could hit it and get away clean. His brother should know that by now.

Chris looked both ways on 5th Avenue. When he saw no sign of life, he placed a metal disc on the door near its handle. The metal disc adhered to the door's lock, centered perfectly against its keyhole, and let out a gentle whine. A second later, its digital display lit up a bright red. Then it turned green with a sudden click, the display rotating one hundred and eighty degrees.

Just like that, the door was unlocked.

"We're in," said Chris.

"You're welcome," said Erich.

"Cameras?" Chris whispered. The annoyance in his voice was a bit more apparent now.

Erich picked up on it and got to work. A second or two later, nearly every light inside the bank shut off. The security cameras followed immediately after.

"Done and done," said Erich in his usual chipper voice.

Chris found himself growing more annoyed by the second. He walked over to the locked gate separating him from the small hallway at the back of the bank. The hall was lined with safe-deposit boxes. Hundreds of the silver containers, each secured with two locks. One keyhole belonged to the bank, the other to the customer. Each box required both keys to be turned for the contents to be removed.

But Chris didn't need either. He had his magic silver disc. Erich had built it six years ago, and it had been a constant source of revenue ever since.

The gate's lock was first. When it clicked open, Chris pushed the gate to the side, walked down the hall, and found box #103. He placed his silver disc on the first keyhole and waited for the light to turn green. Then he did the same with its second keyhole.

With the small metal door unlocked, Chris pulled out the matching metal drawer. He placed it on the center of the table in front of him and reached inside. It was just as the woman in the building next to his had described to her friend — nearly overflowing with antique jewelry. This box alone was the biggest score of Chris Fox's life.

"Can't keep the lights off too much longer," Erich warned through the earpiece. "Residents are already calling the power company."

"Give me a few minutes," Chris said as he slipped the backpack off his shoulders. He dumped the contents of the box inside and looked again at the wall of safe-deposit boxes. "I gotta make this look good."

Chris knew he had to at least empty a dozen or so other boxes if he wanted the robbery to look random and unfocused. He couldn't leave a clue that would lead back to him. Targeting his neighbor's jewelry would certainly be just that.

"You've got ninety seconds," said Erich. "Then the power comes back on."

Chris didn't respond. He was already emptying his third safe-deposit box.

CHAPTER 27

FOX IN TALKS

ParkourSisters: *Hey, what's up?*

saiguy: *Not much. Taking Solo out for a test flight.*

ParkourSisters: *Nice! Did you have any luck adjusting the speed?*

saiguy: *I think so. If it works out, I should get it up to 70 mph.*

ParkourSisters: *That's nuts!*

saiguy: *Nah, Boo. That's science.*

saiguy: *You do any more late-night flying recently?*

ParkourSisters: *Yeah. Just had Hacker out buzzing the park and then brought him back. Nothing special.*

ParkourSisters: *He was keeping me company while I crammed for the PSATs.*

"Parker, time for dinner!" her mom yelled from the next room.

Parker Reading sighed. "Coming!" she yelled back. Then she typed a quick goodbye to Sai Patel into the pop-up window on her computer screen. Without waiting for his reply, she stood up from her desk chair.

Parker knew Sai wouldn't be bothered by her abrupt exit. He was used to it by now. That was sort of the way with SWARM — the Society for Web-Operated Aerial Remote Missions. They were both a part of the group, and Sai knew the habits of its members better than most. He was an avid user of their message boards.

As Parker arched her back, something cracked. She cringed. She had spent too much time in front of the computer today. That would change soon when wrestling practice started up again. Parker was looking forward to it. She was hoping to best her winning season from last year. After all, the only girl on the wrestling team had to keep up appearances. She was trying to be a trailblazer here. Not to mention it was fun to win — super fun.

As she walked out of her room and down the hall past the bathroom, Parker's feet slipped a bit on the old hardwood floor. "Whoa!" she said as she nearly fell into the living room.

"Sorry," said her mom. "I mopped when I got home from work. I might have used too much floor polish."

"You think?" said Parker, smiling at a face that looked so similar to her own.

Both Parker and her mother had long blond hair and thin, athletic frames, and both dressed in T-shirts and jeans whenever possible. If it wasn't for the fact that Parker had a good two inches on her mom and her mom had a few more freckles and wrinkles, they might be mistaken for twins, or sisters at the very least.

Parker's mom found an endless source of joy from people asking if they were sisters. Parker considered it more of an endless source of annoyance. She and her mom were close, but she didn't want to be mistaken for someone who was almost fifty years old. She had a good thirty-four years before she wanted to hear a comment like that.

"I saw that boy again," Mom was saying, "the one with the long hair. He wasn't with anybody, in case you're wondering."

"That is not at all what I was wondering," said Parker.

"Why don't you ask him out sometime?" said her mom. "You're very take-charge. He'd probably be impressed."

"I'm not interested in that guy, Mom. Why don't you date him if you're so into him?"

"I don't think your father would like that."

"It's not like he's ever home."

"Parker!"

"Yeah, yeah," Parker muttered. She went to the refrigerator and poured herself a glass of ice water. "I know."

She didn't want to get into that particular conversation again. Her mom defended her dad no matter what. Yeah, he was busy. Yeah, he was a workaholic. Yeah, he paid the insane mortgage on their tiny little Brooklyn apartment. But her mom worked too. And she still found the time to be home and cook dinner and make it to Parker's wrestling matches and her karate rank tests. Her mom never gave herself enough credit. She was too busy talking up Parker's dad. But Dad was a full-grown man. He could talk himself up. If he was ever home, at least.

"Is this about that little friend from the computer?" her mom asked.

"My little friend?"

"What, is he something *more*?"

"I'm part of an online society, Mom," said Parker, sitting in her chair next to the window. It had been her spot since she was small enough to fit in a high chair. "It's not a dating site."

"Oh, yes," said her mother, making a sarcastic face. "The all-important SWARM! Very serious business."

"Hey, we found the guy who was stealing from that bodega a few months ago," said Parker.

She understood her mom was just teasing, but it was a sensitive topic. Parker was proud of the work she did with SWARM — or Drone Academy, as she loved calling it. Parker had been one of the founders of the tight-knit online group. It was her proudest achievement. Even more so than her black belt in Isshin-Ryu karate and her nearly flawless wrestling record.

"Honey, I'm just pushing your buttons," said her mom.

"And we helped find that family's dog last week. That family in Queens."

"I'm sorry. I shouldn't have teased you."

"We do a lot of good, Mom," Parker said as her mother brought her a white plate with fish, lemon, and a side of asparagus. "And we're getting better every day."

"And I'm sure that boy Howard talks about you as much as you talk about him," Mom said with a wink as she sat down across from Parker.

"I don't want to talk about Howard," said Parker, turning to look out the window.

"That's a first," Mom said. She cut into her fish. "Did you hear about Mrs. Kingsley?"

"Which one is she again?"

"Parker, you're terrible."

"What?" said Parker, digging into her meal now. "There are a lot of old ladies in our building. I can't keep them straight."

"She's the lady whose groceries you help carry," her mom said. "You do it almost every week."

"Oooh," said Parker. "Betty."

"You're on a first name basis with Mrs. Kingsley?" Mom raised an eyebrow as she sipped her water.

"No," said Parker. "I'm on a first name basis with Betty."

"Sigh."

"You can't say the word *sigh*, Mom," said Parker. She had almost completely devoured her fish already. Her mom was still working on her second bite.

"Well, anyway, there was a robbery a few blocks away, at the USofA Bank," Mom continued, spearing her third bite with her fork. "Mrs. Kingsley's —"

"Betty's."

"Fine . . . *Betty's* safe-deposit box was broken into last night. Her entire antique jewelry collection was stolen."

"Oh no!" said Parker. Her voice had changed to one of genuine concern. "She was just telling me about her jewels last week when I was helping her inside. She must have told me that same story a dozen times. She loved that stuff!"

"There were about twenty or so boxes broken into. She was one of the unlucky ones."

"Unless she was the target the whole time."

"Oh, Parker," Mom said, letting out an actual sigh this time. "Is this going to be another of your *missions?*" She used air quotes on the last word to get her meaning across. The gesture was not lost on her daughter.

"Gotta go, Mom," Parker said, standing up. She'd already cleaned her plate. She tended to inhale her food. It was worse when she was excited about something. She took her dishes into the kitchen before heading down the hall back toward her room.

"Say hello to Howard for me!" Mom called after her.

Already in her bedroom, Parker rolled her eyes. "Don't think I didn't hear that!"

CHAPTER 28

FOX AND HAWKS

The metal double doors that led to the basement of 4912 Union Street were open again. The doors had been built at an angle, and through them was a mess of shadows, an old bicycle, and plenty of storage tubs and boxes. They were all belongings that the residents of the building above couldn't possibly fit in their small apartments. In some cases, they were things the residents didn't *want* to fit into their small apartments.

But there were a few prized possessions hiding in the basement's dusty corners. There was a model train belonging to Mrs. Monsivais. A baseball card collection Mr. Valente kept hidden from his wife, who tended to throw anything unnecessary into the garbage. There was an aquarium Mr. Donnelly kept telling himself he'd fill up again any day now.

With all those treasures inside, it made sense that the super, Mr. Petit, hated when Parker accidentally left the basement doors open. But when Parker took her drone out for a spin, she thought of little else but getting her bird into the air. Especially at night, when she was tired from a long day and all she wanted to do was relax in front of her computer.

Besides, no matter how much Mr. Petit hated Parker using the communal basement as her drone launch, he hated her old methods even more.

Before being *reassigned* to the basement, Parker had launched her drone right through her bedroom window. It had taken careful planning to get the launch coordinates correct. She'd finally managed but only after banging the drone into the wall a good dozen times, forcing the super to repair the plaster, a window frame, and even a broken window.

The money for the fixes had come from Parker's own pocket, but Mr. Petit still hadn't been happy. He hadn't been even the least bit impressed when Parker finally succeeded in programming her drone to perfectly avoid the window and wall and return to her desk at the press of a single button on her keyboard.

Parker had opted to store her drone in the basement after that, but had kept the shortcut recall button on her keyboard — just in case. Maybe someday she could convince Mr. Petit to let her launch the drone, affectionately named Hacker, from her room again. And if she was honest, maybe she left the basement doors open on purpose a few times, just to show him the merits of launching from her own apartment. So far, Mr. Petit hadn't gotten the hint.

Everyone in Drone Academy — or SWARM, as they all called it — had named his or her drone. Hacker was named after Parker's number-one pastime. When she wasn't in the dojo or on the wrestling mat, she was in front of her computer, learning new skills or applying old ones. Not everything she did was strictly *legal*, but if she was ever going to work for the government's cyber-defense security team, she needed to get her practice hours in any way she could.

Even now, as Parker piloted her drone via a pre-recorded flight pattern, she was busy trying to find a way into the USofA Bank's computer records. She squinted through her dark-framed glasses at the code that took up half her screen. Then she glanced over at Hacker's cam for a second, watching the live-feed camera but not thinking too much about it for the time being.

Hacker hovered high above the traffic circle near Prospect Park, right down the street from the Reading family's apartment. Parker wasn't sure about the legalities of flying a drone in Brooklyn, so she mostly kept her activity to the park and its surrounding areas. So far it worked. No one seemed to notice the gray, almost bug-like drone. Its green and red flashing lights and six gray helicopter blades didn't draw that much attention. Parker hadn't had any incidents, aside from nearly crashing into a kite or two on a sunny day.

Suddenly, a window popped up on her computer screen.

saiguy: *What's happening?*

ParkourSisters: *Oh, hey. Not much.*

saiguy: *Watching Hacker's GPS signal. Do you ever go anywhere but the park?*

ParkourSisters: *I'm just stretching Hacker's wings. There's something soothing about watching him make rounds when I don't have to pilot.*

saiguy: *The whole point of owning a drone is to fly the thing, Parker.*

ParkourSisters: *Who needs that kind of stress? I just like the view.*

saiguy: *I'm about to take Solo out for a spin. Need my hands free. Switch to audio?*

Parker didn't answer. Instead she pressed a few shortcuts on her keyboard and took her headset out of her desk drawer. She didn't usually *talk* to Sai much. He preferred to instant message whenever possible. From what Parker knew of him — and she knew him pretty well — Sai seemed like the kind of guy who would rather deal with virtual reality than reality itself. Talking on the phone was too much a part of the real world.

"You read me?" Parker said into the black microphone that jutted out of the headset near her cheek.

"Loud and clear," said Sai. "So I know you're hacking right now. That much is obvious."

"No idea what you're talking about," Parker replied.

"Whenever you zone out like you're doing now, you're hacking," said Sai. "Probably into something you shouldn't be hacking into."

"OK, honesty time?"

"Uh-huh."

"I might have cracked open the USofA Bank's secure server."

"*Formerly* secure server," Sai corrected.

"Yep," said Parker.

"You're not turning to the dark side on us all of a sudden, are you?" asked Sai. "Not that I'd be opposed to a few million in a secret, off-shore account . . ."

"This is serious, Sai," said Parker. "One of my neighbors had her safe-deposit box broken into last night. She lost thousands of dollars of jewelry. Maybe more."

"And you're trying to log into the security feed to find out who did it."

"I was," said Parker. "But that's just it — there is no feed. The power was out."

"Somehow, I doubt that was a fluke."

"Yeah, the perp had to be responsible," said Parker. "No question."

She leaned back in her chair and stole another look at Hacker's live feed. He was still flying over Prospect Park, hovering over a fairly secluded stone pond. Parker liked it there. She had taken her laptop out there more times than she could remember.

"So I guess I should dig up the power company's records and see if I can find anything," Parker said, bringing her mind back to the problem at hand.

"I guess that's the next step. The flight cam from last night didn't show anything?"

Parker froze. She had completely forgotten the flight cam. But she didn't want to say that. No way Sai would let that go.

"Did you not have him out last night?" Sai asked after a pause. "Or did you not check the camera feed?" He didn't laugh, but there was certainly amusement in his voice.

Finally, Parker said, "I forgot I had him out, OK? Leave me alone."

Parker always kept Hacker's camera on during flights. She recorded them all and played them back from time to time, sometimes during rough weather when she didn't want to risk taking Hacker outside. That meant there was a recording of last night's flight.

Parker hadn't noticed anything odd while she was studying, but maybe if she was lucky, Hacker had caught the thief on camera near the bank. The way the flight plan was programmed, the drone would have had four, maybe five chances to get the bank in his sights.

"I can't believe you didn't check your own recording!" Sai said, obviously enjoying himself.

"Yeah, yeah," Parker muttered. She wasn't as amused. "I'm checking now . . ."

Sai didn't respond. He was too busy laughing. Once he got started, he had a hard time stopping. Unfortunately for Parker, Sai would be laughing for quite a while yet.

CHAPTER 29

FOX AND LOCKS

12:47 a.m.

Hacker buzzed over the corner of Union Street and 5th Avenue. An old lady pushed a cart full of bags and bottles. Two young people out on a date kissed goodnight on the front stoop of a brownstone. A man in a sanitation worker's uniform limped slowly by, exhausted from a long day's work.

01:47 a.m.

Hacker circled again over Union and 5th. A raccoon popped its head out of a trash can, clutching something shiny in its jaws. A rat scurried across the street, perhaps sensing the drone above.

02:47 a.m.

The wind rustled a few stubborn leaves atop a tree planted in a dirt square, surrounded by sidewalk on all sides. There was no other movement.

Just as Hacker changed course and headed back to Prospect Park, he captured a dark figure standing by the bank's front door. The man was in the shot for only three seconds, but he was there. The man was dressed in a long black winter coat and a matching black ski mask.

As Parker watched, the feed captured the man placing some sort of device on the door. After a moment, it seemed to glow.

* * *

ParkourSisters: *There! What is that?*

saiguy: *I don't see anything. That shadow?*

Parker rolled her eyes. She'd already watched the footage several times, but still. She couldn't believe Sai didn't see it.

ParkourSisters: *Are you even looking at this feed? That's a guy. That's clearly a guy.*

saiguy: *OK . . . oh, wait. OK, you're right.*

ParkourSisters: *Thank you!*

saiguy: *So that's him? That's the culprit?*

ParkourSisters: *I think so. Hold on. I'm going to send the footage to the NYPD.*

Minimizing her chat window on the SWARM boards, Parker pulled up a new window and navigated to the NYPD crime stoppers page. She quickly filled out the form, uploaded the footage from Hacker's camera, and hit the submit button.

ParkourSisters: *There. Done. They have to be able to do something with that.*

saiguy: *I don't know what. You can't make out a thing. Just a shadowy guy in a . . . what is that? A ski mask?*

ParkourSisters: *It's gotta be the perp. The police will be able to make out height, maybe weight from this . . .*

saiguy: *There's nothing here. No real way to identify him.*

ParkourSisters: *OK, but see that little glowing disc?*

saiguy: *Yeah . . . oh. I see what you're saying.*

ParkourSisters: *That's our way in. We don't identify the guy. We identify the tech.*

CHAPTER 30

FOX ON WALKS

"So how's the . . . job hunt going?" Erich asked.

Chris had his phone to his ear as he walked down 7th Avenue, heading to his favorite pizza joint. It wasn't a quick walk, but it was worth it. Fifteen blocks from his apartment was justified when there was good pizza to be had. Quality pizza wasn't as easy to find in New York City as most locals claimed.

Chris had his phone to his ear as he walked. He took a second to smile at the mother pushing a stroller before his face became serious again.

"Not great," said Chris into his phone. "Let's just say he was closed."

"Closed?" Erich said. Chris couldn't see his face, but he knew what expression his brother was making. He'd seen that holier-than-thou look for decades. "Closed for today?"

"Closed forever," said Chris. "We're going to have to find a new guy."

He couldn't say it over the phone, but the *guy* they were referring to was the owner of a pawnshop. Stealing the old lady's jewels was just part of the process. It was the toughest part, sure, but there was more work to be done. After they stole the jewels, they had to find a place to sell them.

The trick was finding the right pawnshop. They needed a store that could pay them close to what the jewelry was worth, but they also needed a store that didn't ask any questions. They needed a place that was discreet enough to not rat them out if the cops came looking.

Chris had lined up just the place. It was a little corner shop in Queens. He'd used the guy for years now without a hiccup. The man had come highly recommended from another local thief. But now there was a major problem. The police had busted the shop just last week.

If he wanted to do business with his contact, Chris would have to wait five to ten years — that's how long it would take for the guy to get out of jail. Chris couldn't wait that long. He needed to sell the jewels soon, which meant he'd have to start his search all over again.

"So," said Erich. He had clearly taken a moment to calm himself down. "Any leads yet?"

"I'll find something," said Chris. His voice was full of confidence. His mind didn't quite match.

"Keep me posted," said Erich. "I got rent to pay, you know."

"I know."

"Oh, and hey, it might be nothing, but I saw something weird last night."

"Yeah?"

"Yeah. Just a blip."

"That doesn't sound good," Chris said. He stopped outside the pizza place. This was the type of conversation you didn't bring inside with you.

"I was looking at the USofA Bank, digging around in their server, and I noticed someone else," said Erich.

"Someone else?" Chris said. "What do you mean *someone else?*"

"Someone else was doing the same thing as me," said Erich. "From the trail he left, it looks like he was poking around the security records."

"So it was a hacker? Is that what you're saying?"

"Yeah," said Erich. "I tried to trace him back to his computer, but he's good. Led me on a couple wild goose chases."

"But he didn't find anything in the records, right? You made sure of that."

"There's no security feed of you to find," Erich assured him. "But I'm still gonna look into this guy. If he's police, we need to know about it."

"OK," said Chris. "Good looking out."

"You just keep hunting for that . . . job, all right?" said Erich. "The sooner we get this stuff gone, the better."

"I'm on it," said Chris. He hung up and dropped the phone into his pocket. Then he pushed open the glass door in front of him. He was on it — but only after a pizza break.

CHAPTER 31

FOX AND CLOCKS

"I know it," said Howard To, smiling at Parker through the screen.

Parker smiled back. She liked his smile. He didn't do it as much as he should.

Howard was Vietnamese-American and had dark eyes and hair, a far different look than Parker's light-toned everything. His coloring was just another of his qualities that contrasted with Parker. She was athletic; Howard looked like he hadn't worked out a day in his life. She was often referred to as peppy; Howard was overly sarcastic. Her heroes were real-life athletes or computer geniuses; Howard's waved swords around or cast magical spells in comic books. But despite all these differences, Howard — or HowTo, going by his screen name — was Parker's favorite person to talk with. Not just out of the SWARM members, either. Out of almost anyone.

"So?" said Parker, looking directly at her webcam. "Don't leave me in suspense."

"It's a digital readout display from an iFound timer. It's not something you'd see on a lock-pick device or whatever the heck that is. That's a custom job," Howard said.

"So where would I start looking for something like that?"

"The Internet," said Howard. "That's a really specific, discontinued piece of junk tech. I only know, like, two stores that would even stock it online."

"And you're sending links to those stores to me now?"

Howard playfully rolled his eyes. "No, I'm video chatting with you."

"Well, when you stop gazing into my dreamy eyes you're going to send me those links, right?"

"Jeez," said Howard with a grin. "You make it so appealing."

With a wink — Parker had never seen him wink — Howard signed off from their video chat. Less than a minute later, Parker's computer pinged with an email alert.

She opened the email and clicked on the link. As the page loaded, Parker looked at Hacker's live feed. The drone was over 7th Avenue now, on his way back to the park. He was almost over that pizza place she liked.

A few minutes later, Parker had successfully found a back door into the first website Howard had sent. She began riffling through the site's digital sales records. Much to her surprise, she came up with a sale for the iFound timer almost instantly. It had been sent to a post office box in Manhattan.

This could very well be the guy, Parker realized. The digital display hadn't been sent to a personal address. That in and of itself raised a little suspicion.

As Hacker passed over 7th and then 8th Avenues, Parker continued to type. With a little above-board searching, she discovered that the PO Box was registered to a business: E-Rock, Inc., This felt right. Something about this felt like it made sense.

Parker opened a new window on her screen and began to work her magic. The post office in question would have security cameras. It was time to find out if the owner of E-Rock, Inc. wore a black winter jacket.

CHAPTER 32

FOX AND CROCKS

Erich Fox hung up his phone. His brother wasn't even answering his calls now. That meant one of two things — either Chris had spent the entire day on the subway, or he couldn't find a pawnshop to sell the jewels. The second choice seemed the most likely.

Chris didn't seem to be taking this setback too seriously. To him, it was a small bump in the road, a tiny obstacle that he'd eventually overcome. To Erich, it was different. This was watching a plan, one that had been weeks in the making, fall apart. This was technology *years* in the making being wasted on a heist with no endgame.

Sometimes Erich had a hard time sympathizing with his brother or even finding a common ground. They were so different. Sure, they were both stubborn. They'd inherited that from their dad. But for years now, Erich had felt like he was doing the lion's share of the work. Chris was the legwork guy. He took the physical risks. But Erich designed all the tech that made their heists possible in the first place. And it was Erich who kept a digital eye on things both before and after each crime.

Erich frowned as he thought about it. He scratched the short, scruffy patch of hair on his head. Here he was doing all this work, putting in all this effort, and Chris was only there for the hour or so each crime took to commit. Chris kept claiming he was street smart, but what did he really contribute? And now Chris couldn't even be bothered to answer his calls?

Erich was so lost in thought that he walked right past the post office. When he finally realized his mistake, he stopped, turned around, and walked back toward the old building. It was time to get to work. He popped the collar on his favorite denim jacket, the one with the crocodile logo on the back. Then he headed inside the post office.

It was true, Erich was the real reason for his family's successful criminal activities. But maybe if he possessed the street smarts Chris was always talking about, he might have noticed the gray drone hovering above the lamppost at the corner of the block.

* * *

"There's our man now!" Parker said into her headset.

"Nice!" said Howard. "So he's the guy you found on the bank's security feed?"

"Yep," said Parker.

"But you don't actually know he's the bank robber yet, right?"

"Well, no," Parker admitted as she stared at her computer monitor. "But I checked both websites you sent me. He's the only person who ordered that digital display. At least, he was the only person in all of New York, New Jersey, or any of the surrounding states."

"Yeah, it's not a popular piece of tech."

"Lucky for us," Parker said. "I checked the post office's feed, and this guy — the owner of E-Rock, Inc. — comes in every Wednesday about this time. He checks his PO Box and then heads home. Or at least I'm guessing that's where he goes."

"And that's why you have Hacker out today?"

"Yep," said Parker. "Gonna follow this sucker home."

Howard didn't say anything. Parker figured he was looking at the live feed she was sending him on his computer. He was looking for their target, just like she was.

Less than a minute later, the owner of the E-Rock PO Box stepped out of the building and squinted in the bright sunlight. Then he turned right to walk back in the direction he'd come from.

For the first time, Parker noticed the green crocodile on the back of the man's denim jacket. It wasn't the black coat from the robbery, that was for sure. But this crocodile man was the only lead she had.

"OK, HowTo, I'm gonna have to lose you," Parker said.

"But we just now found each other in this lifetime," said Howard. It was a cute comment. A bit goofier than something Howard would usually say but cute nonetheless.

"I need my hands free," said Parker. "Clicking off."

"Until we meet again," Howard said in an overly dramatic voice.

Parker didn't respond. The E-Rock guy would get too much of a lead if she wasn't careful. She had just enough time to give Howard a quick laugh before clicking the end button.

CHAPTER 33

FOX DOWN BLOCKS

Parker was careful to keep her distance. She held Hacker half a block back from the man in the crocodile jacket at all times. Using the zoom feature, she kept the camera focused on him and kept the course as steady as she could using her handheld gaming controller rather than her keyboard. For extra safety, she stayed high enough in the air to avoid power lines. Fortunately, she didn't have to worry about the drone being detected due to noise — Hacker wasn't particularly quiet, but neither were New York City streets.

The man in the crocodile jacket turned the corner, and a few seconds later, Hacker turned the corner after him. Parker breathed a sigh of relief when she quickly located her target again. She was lucky he wasn't on to her. If the man started running, she might not be able to keep up.

Parker wasn't the pilot that some of her fellow SWARM members were. Sai had his speed drone and VR goggles. Zora Michaels, the only other female member, had an almost superhuman reaction time and piloting skills that bordered on instinctual. And Howard, he was the most determined out of all of them. He was willing to take chances and make modifications to his drone whenever the situation demanded it. Parker had a hard time understanding why he never bothered to take chances in his personal life.

While Parker was daydreaming about her friends at SWARM, the man in the crocodile jacket had walked several more blocks before turning another corner. Parker got her head back in the game and turned the corner after him, narrowly avoiding a fire escape that had no business being where it was.

She scanned the alleyway below. There was nothing. No man, no reptilian jacket, nothing. Parker felt a tinge of panic travel up her spine. She'd lost him.

Just then there was movement at the very bottom of the screen. Parker panned the camera down slightly and saw a door closing. It was the back entrance to what looked like an apartment complex of some kind.

With the man in the crocodile jacket now safely out of viewing range, Parker lowered Hacker until he was parallel with the door. The closer inspection revealed the number 21 on the door. This wasn't an entrance to an entire apartment building —it was the way into one particular basement apartment.

If this man was the culprit, Parker had just discovered his home address. And the best news was, the suspect had no idea that anyone was on his tail.

Parker smiled as she typed in the command for Hacker to return to his charging base in her building's basement. Then she opened a new chat window. She had to tell Howard the good news.

* * *

Erich Fox continued to look out of his apartment's peephole. The drone that had been following him for blocks had grown bolder. Erich had noticed its green and red lights and gray spinning blades a few blocks after he'd left the post office. The drone was now hovering right outside, its camera pointed right at his door. He wondered if it could see through his peephole.

Before he could think too much about it, the drone swiveled, rose into the air, and flew out of sight. It was probably heading home — or worse, Erich thought, it could be hovering above the building, waiting for him to leave again.

Erich stood completely still, letting his fear slowly transform into pure rage. Then in a huff, he stormed over to his computer and powered it on.

CHAPTER 34

FOX AND JOCKS

Parker was exhausted. Karate class had gone long, and it was a sparring night. Sparring nights were always harder than kata nights. No matter how many times or at what speed Parker practiced her katas, they were still just a prearranged set of kicks, punches, and stances. They weren't the cardio workout that sparring was.

Parker sighed as she dried her hair in the bathroom. She was happy to have washed off the hour's worth of sweat, but she could already feel new beads forming on her forehead in the hot bathroom. Even her lightweight sweatpants and her old white T-shirt felt too hot.

As Parker exited the room, she nearly collided with her mother. Mom was busy putting a diamond earring in one ear and attempting to put a high-heeled shoe on one foot at the same time. Luckily, despite every part of her body aching, Parker still managed to dodge her mom and sidestep out of the way in time to avoid a collision.

"Hey now!" Parker said.

"Sorry, sugar," said her mom. "I'm already late meeting your father."

"I could have sworn you two had already met," said Parker. She was never too tired for one-liners.

"Anniversary dinner, remember?" Mom said on her way to the kitchen.

"Oops!" called Parker after her mom. "Happy anniversary!" She followed her mom into the kitchen but at a much slower pace. Mom was now attempting to zip up the slim-fitting black dress she was wearing.

"Thanks, kiddo," Mom said. "And no worries. It's not your anniversary, after all."

Parker zipped the dress up the rest of the way. Her mom mouthed a silent "thank you" and then opened the refrigerator, retrieving a bottle of water.

"You set for the night? We probably won't be back until late."

"I'll heat up a frozen pizza or something," said Parker. "I'm gonna crash in front of my computer anyway."

Mom unscrewed the cap from her bottle of water and took a hearty swig. She looked almost as winded as Parker had been just an hour ago. Then she headed toward the front door, grabbing a small purse that matched her dress. She was about to leave when she paused and glanced at Parker. "You OK?" she asked.

"Yeah, just tired," said Parker. "Karate was grueling."

"They had you fight that third-degree black belt again, didn't they? You keep your guard up this time?"

"Mom, you're going to be late," said Parker, opening the front door. "I mean, even later."

"Always keep your guard up," her mom said with a smile. Then she walked through the doorway, giving Parker a kiss on the cheek at the same time.

"Good night," Parker said.

"Night, Parker," Mom said. And then as quickly as she had appeared, her mother was gone.

Parker peered down the dimly lit hallway of her apartment building. The super had time to complain about her drone, but no time to change a light bulb once in a while?

Parker shut the door and flipped the top and bottom locks. Then she walked over to the kitchen and pulled a boxed pizza out of the freezer. Nothing like a healthy dinner to complement a healthy workout.

She slid the pizza out of its packaging and then into the oven, not bothering to preheat it. After setting the oven to three hundred and fifty degrees, Parker walked back down the hallway to her room, a fresh glass of water in hand. Time to see what the SWARM gang was up to.

* * *

"You sure you got the address right?" Chris said into his phone. He shivered as he walked down the street. It was colder outside than he had anticipated.

"Yeah, I'm sure," said Erich. "Some of us are good at our jobs."

"Pfft," Chris said, dismissing his brother's comment. "So this guy, you think he got us on film?"

"The night of the —?" Erich started to say when Chris interrupted.

"Cell phones, remember," Chris warned. "Let's keep the details to a minimum."

"The night of the . . . incident?" Erich said instead. "I don't know. All I can think is that maybe he got me on camera leaving the post office. That's the first time I noticed the drone. And that's the PO Box I used when I ordered all of the parts to make the . . . device."

"So tell me again how you found him," said Chris.

"I've already told you three times," said Erich.

"Pretend I'm as stupid as you think I am."

Erich sighed. Then finally, he said, "It took some doing, but I managed to track his IP address back through the bank's website. I caught him digging around in the security camera files."

"Right."

"Once I had that, I looked into some feeds nearby — an ATM camera on the corner, the security camera outside the apartment next door. That's how I spotted the drone. The same one that was following me outside the post office."

"I just don't get how this guy lives so close to me," Chris said into the phone.

"I told you we shouldn't have hit a place right around the corner from where you live," said Erich.

"Cell phones," Chris said again, noticeably more annoyed this time.

"All right, take a look in front of you, Mr. High Security," Erich said.

Chris did. From his position on the sidewalk he could see two rusted doors at the bottom of the building. They led down to the basement of 4912 Union Street, two buildings down from his own.

"At least there's easy access," said Erich.

"I'm going in," said Chris. "Cell phone silence until I call you in an hour. Somebody's gotta clean up your mess."

"*My* mess?" Erich said.

But he was wasting his breath. Chris had already hung up.

CHAPTER 35

FOX WHO STALKS

Parker finally made it to her desk chair, but it took a Herculean effort. Every one of her muscles ached. Even her brain felt like mush. She needed sleep, but Parker was a night owl. She was sure a second wind was coming.

On her desk sat a smoldering, formerly frozen pizza. Parker picked up a slice and bit into it, instantly regretting not waiting. It was still way too hot. Now her gums were on the list of body parts that hurt.

Without getting up, Parker managed to lean over and open her window, hoping the light from her computer screen and small desk lamp wouldn't attract any moths or other flying critters. She had removed her window screen months ago to accommodate Hacker, and hadn't bothered to replace it. The rest of her lights were off, though, so hopefully she wouldn't have to deal with any unannounced visitors.

The computer made its triumphant loading sound, and Parker began to pay attention to it. She logged into the

SWARM website to see who else was online tonight. At the same time, she opened her drone navigation program. She had made sure the basement doors were open tonight on her way home from karate. Hacker had been waiting patiently for her go command ever since.

Surprisingly, no one was on the SWARM site. Parker had been hoping to talk to Sai or Howard about the case. Now that Hacker was freshly charged, she planned to take him back into New York City. She'd set up a stakeout outside the apartment of the crocodile man and would hopefully catch him heading somewhere.

Tailing him had been more fun than Parker had originally thought. Now if only she could catch him in the act of something illegal. If she was really lucky, maybe he would try to sell the jewels he had stolen. No matter what he did, Parker would have some new information on him. And information was the most valuable commodity.

Parker had already typed the man's address into Hacker's programming. He would fly to that destination using his map navigation feature, giving Parker some free time to do a little sleuthing of her own. She and Hacker were becoming a better team every day. It was the perfect working relationship — he did the legwork, and she did the thinking.

* * *

Chris Fox was trying not to think about his brother as he made his way through the dark basement of 4912 Union

Street. His mind was focused on the job at hand. He was going to find the other hacker. He wasn't sure what he was going to do when he found him, but it wasn't going to be pretty.

As Chris placed one foot on the bottom of the wooden staircase that led up to the building's first floor, something moved in the corner of his eye. He snapped his head to the side just in time to see red and green lights flashing in some sort of bizarre sequence. Then there was the sound of fan blades and the hum of something that sounded like a motor.

None of it made any sense until the shadowy thing lifted into the air. It was the drone Erich had tracked. But it wasn't moving toward Chris — it was heading for the double doors. A moment later, the drone flew out of the basement.

After the thing was gone, Chris let out a sigh of relief. He'd debated shutting the doors but hadn't wanted to draw any attention to himself. Apparently that had been exactly the right call.

Putting his mind back to the task in front of him, Chris continued up the stairs. Erich had said the apartment he was looking for was 3B.

* * *

Parker jumped when she heard the sound at the front door. Then she calmed herself. It was just the doorknob. Mom and Dad were probably back early.

She headed out of her bedroom and walked down the hall toward the door. All the while, the doorknob rattled.

Did they forget their keys? Parker wondered. *I thought Mom grabbed hers when she left.*

She was nearly at the door when she heard a low electronic whine. It wasn't a noise Parker had ever heard before. She looked out the peephole, but she didn't see her mother's face smiling back at her or her father fumbling for his keychain. She saw a man with a shaved head, a goatee, and . . . a black coat.

Parker did her best to hold her gasp in as she stepped away from the door. She'd been so busy tracking the bank robber, she hadn't even considered the possibility that *he* was capable of tracking *her.*

As she stood there, there was a sickening *click* from the door. It had unlocked itself, as easily as if the man on the other side had a key. The electronic whine sounded again. He was working on the bolt lock now.

Parker wanted to run. She wanted to scream. She wanted to grab her phone from her desk and call the police. But instead, she was frozen in place. She felt like she couldn't move. This was what all those years of martial-arts training had gotten her.

She was a deer in the headlights — and the man in the coat was an oncoming truck.

CHAPTER 36

FOX HITS ROCKS

"Do you need help, young man?" said a woman in the hallway.

Chris turned around to see someone much older than he expected. She had gray hair and glasses so thick they couldn't possibly do her any good.

"No, ma'am," Chris said, practicing his kindest smile. "I'm good. Just having trouble with the lock."

"Are you a friend of the Readings?" the woman asked. "Such a nice family."

Chris did his best to maintain his smile. Apparently he was in the middle of a conversation now.

"Oh, wait," she said. "I know you. You live in the building two doors down."

Chris had no idea what to say. This wasn't a good development.

"I think you have me confused with someone else," he finally replied. "I'm staying with the Readings this week."

Despite the lie, his voice seemed calm. He sounded natural and authentic.

"Oh," said the old woman. "You're probably right, then. My eyesight isn't what it used to be."

"Whose is?" Chris said.

The woman smiled at the thought. "You have a nice night now," she said as she shuffled past him. "Don't let those tricky locks get the better of you."

"I'll do my best, ma'am," Chris said. He continued to smile at her until she had made her way down the hall and turned the corner to the stairwell. It seemed to take hours.

Once she was out of sight, Chris turned back to the door. He placed the disc above the bolt lock again and watched it glow.

* * *

Hearing the conversation through the door hadn't calmed Parker's nerves. But when she heard the lock click open, enough was enough. She finally unfroze. There was no time to waste.

Moving as quickly and silently as she could, Parker sprinted down the hallway and into her room. She had her door closed and locked by the time the front door opened behind her.

Now all she had to do was come up with a plan.

* * *

Chris Fox walked into the apartment. He didn't bother to say anything. He didn't yell down the hall to see if anyone was home. He wanted whatever element of surprise he could muster.

He looked in the kitchen and at the small eating nook next to it. The lights were all off. There was no one there. Chris continued in. No one in the living room. No one in the dark hallway. He moved to the bathroom and flipped the light switch. Again, it was empty.

There were two other doors down the hall, likely leading to bedrooms. But Chris was looking for a master hacker, and it wasn't that late. His brother had said this man kept crazy hours. If he was home, surely he'd still be awake.

Chris swung open the door on the left first. It was as dark as the rest of the apartment. He switched on the lights. There was a king-size bed in the center of the room. There was a dresser and a lounge chair but no people.

Chris paused when he noticed the small nightstand next to the bed. There was a photo on it. In the picture stood a man, presumably his wife, and a daughter.

This master hacker was a family man, Chris realized. It made what he had to do all the more difficult. But the hacker had brought this on himself. He'd poked his digital head where it didn't belong.

Shutting the door behind him, Chris reached across the hallway and gripped the other bedroom's doorknob. It was locked. He tried it again, but it didn't budge.

Chris was about to reach for the silver disc in his coat pocket when he heard a sound from the other side of the door. It was a small noise, no more than the shuffling of feet. But there was no doubt about it, Chris was not alone in this apartment.

The break-in had taken much too long already. He couldn't afford to waste another second. The person behind the door had probably already called the cops. The hacker knew he was here.

Chris braced himself and rammed the door with his shoulder. It collapsed inward more easily than he had expected. He nearly lost his balance as he stumbled into the room. A second later, something collided with his face.

It took Chris a few seconds to notice the searing pain. He touched his fingers to his nose and looked down at his hand. There was blood. Someone had just punched him.

His eyes adjusted, focusing on the small person standing squarely in front of him. It was a blond girl, a high schooler at best. There she stood, her fists raised like a prize fighter.

Chris was so stunned that it took him a second to process what had happened. Had the hacker escaped? This coward had left his teenage daughter to fend for herself? What a scumbag.

But when he looked from the girl to the computer situated on her desk the truth hit him, almost as hard as her fist had. There was a live aerial feed running. Another pop-up box displayed computer code.

Chris looked at the girl again. *"You?"* he said. "You're the hacker?"

"No," the girl said, looking over at her window. "He's over there."

* * *

As Parker watched, the intruder moved toward the window she had pointed to. It led out onto a fire escape.

Parker froze in place, still in her fighting position, and held her breath. She had no idea if her timing would work.

At exactly that moment, Hacker came home. The recall program was still operational. The drone navigated his way perfectly through Parker's window, avoiding the wall and glass, just as she'd programmed him. But Hacker didn't avoid the head of the man standing in Parker's apartment.

Just as suddenly as he had broken down her door, the intruder was lying on Parker's floor, unconscious, with a half-broken drone resting on his face.

CHAPTER 37

FOX IN STOCKS

saiguy: *I don't believe you.*

ParkourSisters: *It's true. It happened.*

saiguy: *You can keep saying that, but I still won't believe you. How long?*

ParkourSisters: *Ten minutes.*

saiguy: *You Skyped with Zora for ten full minutes?*

ParkourSisters: *At least.*

saiguy: *Man, you are just full of wins this week.*

ParkourSisters: *To be fair, she was at a coffee shop. She still doesn't want me making fun of her way-too-pink bedroom.*

saiguy: *So how's the aftermath now that you put the notorious Fox brothers in the clink?*

ParkourSisters: *Normal people don't say the word* clink *in real life.*

saiguy: *I'm not normal people.*

ParkourSisters: *You can say that again. Things are good. It took some quick thinking to explain how Chris Fox found me,* *and Mom says she's never letting me out of her sight again. But I haven't had too much to worry about since the cops followed my anonymous tip and caught Erich Fox on that train headed for Connecticut.*

saiguy: *You impress me, Parker. And I don't impress easily.*

ParkourSisters: *That's funny. Zora said the same thing.*

"Parker!" Mom shouted from down the hall. "Hurry it up!"

That was the third time she'd yelled already. If Parker didn't answer her soon, she was afraid her mom would panic and try to break down her newly repaired bedroom door.

"Coming, Mom!" she called. She signed off with Sai and was about to shut down her computer when the machine pinged again. She looked at the screen. Howard was IM'ing her.

"Honey," Parker's mom said as she cracked open the door and stuck her head through. "Your father's outside in the car. He's double parked, and we have dinner reservations in fifteen minutes."

"I'm coming," said Parker. She tried to make eye contact with her mom, but Mom was looking at Parker's computer screen instead.

"Is that Howard?"

"Moooom," Parker said, rolling her eyes as hard as humanly possible.

"You know what," Mom said, "I'm going to tell your father to drive around the block a few times. You two have your little chat."

"He can't even hear you, and I'm completely embarrassed," Parker called as her mom left the room.

But as she typed on her keyboard, Parker was smiling.

* * *

It had taken only two weeks for the new inmate to get to know the guard stationed at the far end of the prison yard. As it turned out, they were both from the same neighborhood . . . or at least that's how the inmate told it.

He would keep chatting with the guard every day or so from now on. Soon, he'd feel comfortable enough with the man to bring up the possibility of the guard delivering him a package. The inmate would bide his time and locate the least complicated lock on the fence of the yard. And after a few bribes, he would have his silver disc in his hand once more.

No matter what, the inmate would give no indication of his plan. He was too smart for that. After all, Chris Fox knew that was how you got caught.

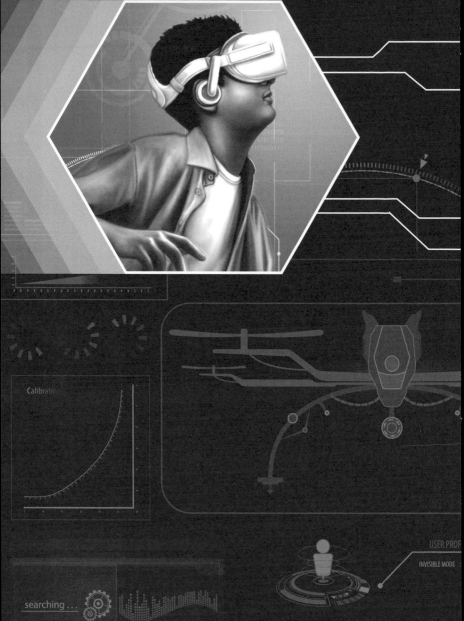

OPERATION
COPYCAT

90%
LOADING

CHAPTER 38

THE FALL OF EILEEN WU

Yesterday

Eileen Wu didn't know how much longer she could hold on. She couldn't find a footing for her right foot. Her left foot was supporting most of her weight, even if it only had a three-inch ledge to stand on. She was clinging to the root above her head, but it was getting harder every second. The root was dirty, and her hands were sweaty. She kept slipping down little by little.

Eileen looked over her shoulder. Below her was at least a six-story drop. She suddenly remembered reading on the Internet that humans can only hope to survive a four-story fall. Anything more was virtually impossible to live through.

As she looked down the cliff face at the waves breaking on the rocks below, Eileen wished she didn't know that fact. But more than anything, she wished she hadn't gone hiking at all today.

Everything had started out normally enough. Eileen had told her mom she was heading to Travels Island, a nature preserve about an hour away from her home in Savannah, Georgia, to do some hiking. She'd put on her favorite pair of capris, the ones with the rugged knee patches that could take a fall. She'd brought her phone, just in case she needed to make an emergency call, and so she could listen to music. And most importantly, she'd packed a backpack full of the essentials: snacks, a book, more snacks, a water bottle, a sweatshirt in case it got cold, and a few more snacks. Then she'd taken off in her little red pickup truck in search of good views, some exercise that didn't feel like it, and a quiet place to sit and relax.

She thought she had found the perfect spot at the top of the cliff. It was an amazing view of the Atlantic Ocean, and the sound of waves hitting shore always relaxed her. While she planned to get through a few chapters of her new book, she had a feeling she'd end up asleep beside the trail. Either way, Eileen decided she'd better snap a few pictures of the view before she forgot to brag about it on social media.

As it turned out, the earth closer to the cliff's edge wasn't as solid as that of the trail. Eileen found that out when she took one step too many toward the view. The ground gave way, and her foot followed. Her leg went next, and the rest of her didn't take much time to catch up.

The next thing she knew, she was dangling from a tree root that jutted out from the cliff face. Eileen had grabbed it instinctively as she fell. She had been hanging from this root ever since. At this point, it felt like hours.

Eileen felt the cramping in her foot. It was getting worse. She couldn't stand on this little ledge for much longer. Her hands felt sweatier than ever. But she had to hang on. She had reason to hope.

About ten minutes ago, Eileen had noticed a boat. For a while, she'd been able to see it over her shoulder when she strained. It was close enough to the shore to have spotted her. She was sure of it.

She checked again now. The boat wasn't there, but surely it had seen her. Surely someone onboard had called the coast guard or the police or the fire department or whomever you called for this sort of thing. It *had* to have seen her. Eileen couldn't afford to think otherwise.

She only had one job now — to hang on until someone came. Someone had to come. She had to believe that.

Then she heard the buzzing sound. At first she mistook it for an insect. Eileen almost cried with frustration. The last thing she needed was another distraction, another bit of misfortune to torture her.

But the buzzing was too loud to be a bug, she realized after a moment. And it was only getting louder.

Eileen looked over her right shoulder and then her left. That's when she saw the little white drone.

She had seen drones before at the mall. There was a guy there who demonstrated how they worked. He'd fly them over the shoppers and impress little kids in the hopes of breaking down their parents and nabbing a sale. This one was different, though. It had a cell phone in its center, almost like its four little white blades were built around the phone.

As it zipped closer to her, Eileen realized it was faster than those drones at the mall too. This wasn't some sixty-dollar toy. This was a piece of expensive equipment.

"Help!" she shouted when it got close enough. If the drone had a phone, that meant it had a camera. It had to be navigating somehow. "Call for help!" she yelled. "Please!"

But the little white drone didn't seem to call anyone. It didn't go get help. Instead, it just stayed there, watching her.

Eileen yelled and screamed at the drone, but it remained where it was, just three feet away from her, hovering in midair. She felt a new sharp pain in the ball of her foot, and her hands slipped another inch. Her screams grew louder.

It wasn't until Eileen stopped screaming that she heard the other new sound. It was similar to the noise that the little white drone's rotating blades made but much louder.

She recognized it almost immediately. It was the sound of a helicopter.

Eileen looked over her shoulder. She felt instant relief. There it was, a rescue chopper. The boat had seen her after all and had sent help. Or maybe this little white drone was her savior. It didn't matter now. The chopper was coming closer, and in a few minutes, she'd be safely flying home.

But for some reason, when Eileen looked back over her shoulder again, the helicopter hadn't moved. It hadn't gotten any closer. She looked over at the little white drone. It hadn't moved either.

Just then she remembered something else she'd read on the Internet, maybe a year ago. A rescue effort had to be called off because a nosy drone had flown too close to the scene. The pilot of the chopper was worried that the drone could get caught in his blades and wreck the helicopter.

Was that what was happening now? she wondered. Why wasn't the little white drone leaving? Why was it just hovering there, staring at her?

Eileen glanced back over her shoulder and screamed when she realized the helicopter was leaving. She yelled, and she screamed, and tears formed in the corners of her eyes. But the little white drone just stayed there, watching her all the while. And her hands slipped another inch.

CHAPTER 39

EVERYONE WAS YELLING

One year ago

Sai Patel sat at his desk, looked at his computer monitor, and stretched out the piece of chewing gum he was holding in between his teeth. It was his worst habit, and he tried not to do it when anyone else was around. But he liked to see how far he could stretch the stuff. It reminded him of playing with silly putty as a little kid.

In front of him on his computer screen was the logo he'd just finished. In large, stylized letters it read, *SWARM*.

Sai smiled as he used a bit of coding to insert the logo as the header for the new website. SWARM. The Society for Web-Based Aerial Remote Missions. Or as his friend and fellow member Parker Reading called it, Drone Academy. As soon as Sai published his work, the site would be finished.

This was it. This was the biggest event in Sai's fifteen-year-old life. He was finally going to be able to contribute something to the world. He was going to turn his hobby of drone piloting into something more.

Another pop-up window opened on his screen. Sai watched as the members logged in, one by one. Finally all eight members were there and accounted for. All Sai had to do was press enter, and the site would go live. And so he did.

* * *

Today

Sai Patel sat at his same desk, looked at his same computer monitor, and stretched a different piece of chewing gum out from his teeth. It was almost eight o'clock in the evening. The SWARM meeting was about to begin.

Parker was the first to log in. Sai saw her screen name, ParkourSisters, appear below his on the list of active users. He wondered what one-liners the peppiest member of SWARM had in her pocket for tonight. She was a consistent source of amusement for Sai. And she was interesting too — a weird mix of native New Yorker, feminist martial artist, and computer nerd.

Sai had never met anyone like Parker. Although, technically, he'd never met her or any of the SWARM members in real life. They all lived in different corners of the country.

Soon, Howard To's screen name, HowTo, appeared. Howard was SWARM's resident know-it-all. He lived with his parents in California, somewhere near Hollywood, if Sai was remembering correctly. Howard was around the same age as Sai — all the members were — but Howard was super smart. It was like he'd outgrown high school as soon as he'd set foot in it.

Almost immediately after Howard, Zora Michaels — Zor_elle, as her screen name stated — entered the site. Zora was another odd mix. At first she seemed like a girly girl from Indiana, decked out in every shade of pink sold at expensive boutiques. But she was the best pilot of the whole group. She flew her drone like she'd been doing it since she learned to walk. Plus she was into comic books. She was a cool kid at her school but one who was big on secret identities.

Sai plugged in his headset. He preferred instant messaging to actually talking, but for group meetings, they almost always chatted via conference call. He couldn't remember how that tradition had started. If Sai had to guess, it had probably been Parker's idea. She was really into putting a personal touch on things, even if no one else wanted it. Zora still refused to Skype with her, but Parker didn't seem like she was going to give up on that goal anytime soon.

As soon as he had his headphones on, Sai regretted it. There was yelling — so much yelling.

"What were you thinking?" Zora yelled, as if directly into his ear.

"I just put my headphones on," Sai said. "Who is she screaming at?"

"You, you moron!" shouted Parker. That greeting was new. Sai didn't really care for it.

"Me?" he said. "What did I do?"

"Are you serious?" Howard said. Everyone was piling on now. "You were all over the news, Sai."

"I was?" Sai said. He was more confused than ever.

"Well, not you exactly," said Howard. "Solo."

Howard was right. Solo wasn't Sai exactly, but he might as well be. Solo was Sai's drone. The little white machine was his hobby, his precious baby, his escape from reality. He had spent so much money and time working on Solo over the years that the drone was like a family member to him.

"Someone explain this to me," said Sai.

"You could have killed that girl!" Zora said. She was still yelling. Sai wished she would stop with all the yelling already.

"What girl?" he finally yelled back.

"The paper said her name was Eileen Wu," Parker replied. "Can we still call it a paper if I'm talking about an Internet article? Would the proper term be paperless?"

"This isn't the time, Parker," said Howard.

"If not now, then when?" Somehow Parker was joking through all of this. "When?" she demanded, louder now.

"This is serious!" said Zora. It wasn't quite a yell this time. It was more of a shout, which almost seemed like progress to Sai. "You were out flying your drone near some nature preserve yesterday. And instead of getting out of the way to let the rescue team do their job, you chose to keep hovering by that poor girl and making your stupid Internet video."

"Would everyone just listen to me?" said Sai. "I didn't have Solo out at all yesterday. My parents dragged me to my little cousin's birthday party. I was in downtown Savannah, at a terrible knockoff pizza place with creepy, animatronic mice who sang to us for the better part of two hours!"

The explanation came out in one breath. Sai typed fast and spoke faster. It only got worse when he was angry.

"That doesn't make any sense," said Zora. She was calmer now. She obviously wanted to believe her friend. "You posted it on your YouTube channel two hours ago."

"Posted what?" Sai asked.

"The video of that Eileen girl," said Zora. "The thing's gone viral."

Sai paused. This was too much. He needed to find out what was going on.

"I'll call you back," was all he said as he clicked out of the chat room.

CHAPTER 40

MOVING TARGETS

Six months ago

Sai tried to be as quiet as possible when he opened the front door to his modest one-story house. The last thing he wanted was for his dad to hear him coming in. He needed to get to his room, change into a new shirt, and soak the old one in the bathroom sink. Hopefully the stain would come right out.

He also needed to clean up his face while he was at it. His dad tended to make a big deal when he saw blood.

"Hi, Sai!" a voice said behind him. It was only the first part of the familiar greeting. "What's up, guy?"

Sai turned around, pretending to scratch his nose with his whole hand. His neighbor, Mr. Morris, was going on eighty years old and losing his hearing, but his eyesight was still twenty-twenty. He didn't even own a pair of glasses. Certainly not one with a prescription as strong as Sai's.

"Hey, Mr. Morris," said Sai.

"Mr. Morris was my dad's name," said Mr. Morris. "And he's long dead. How many times I gotta tell you? You call me Maury."

"There's not really much difference," said Sai.

"Maybe to you, son," said Maury Morris. "What's the matter?"

"What?" said Sai. "Nothing."

"You just always stand around with your hand on your face like that?" the old man asked, walking closer to Sai.

"Just . . ." Sai trailed off, stalling for time. "I just got a bloody nose at school."

"Just like that, huh?" said Mr. Morris. "This the sort of problem you can deal with yourself? Or do you need a crazy old kook butting in?"

"I'm dealing with it," said Sai.

"OK . . . as long as we're still on for Friday," said Mr. Morris. "You know they're not gonna let me drive myself to the doughnut shop."

"We're still on for Friday," Sai said.

He had driven Mr. Morris to the bakery every weekend since he'd gotten his learner's permit. It was the least he could do. Mr. Morris wasn't a relative, but the mischievous old guy might as well have been. He'd practically helped raise Sai. He was the closest thing to a grandfather Sai had.

Without waiting for a response, Sai turned around and rushed through the front door. Mr. Morris was practically family, but he had also just really hurt Sai's chances of getting inside unnoticed.

Fortunately, there was no sign of Dad in the kitchen. He was probably working in his office. He probably had another crazy deadline and was busy furiously graphic designing. Sai wasn't sure that graphic design could be turned into a verb, but it sounded good enough. After all, he had other problems to deal with at the moment.

Sai splashed his face with water and used a tissue to remove the dried blood clinging to his nose and lip. He adjusted his dark hair in the mirror, even though he knew he wasn't going anywhere for the rest of the night. It was more of a reflex than anything.

When Jeff had punched him on the bus, it hadn't really hurt. What bothered Sai was the fact that his nose hadn't stopped bleeding for nearly the entire ride home. He'd just bought this red-and-white striped polo shirt. And now it was redder than anyone at the store had intended. He soaked it in the sink, but looking at it now, he knew it was a lost cause. Another expensive piece of clothing ruined by school bullies.

At least they hadn't broken his glasses again. That was something to be grateful for. Sai had splurged on a brand-name pair this time, dark-framed and thick. He'd noticed an Indian detective wearing a nearly identical pair in a crime drama he watched on TV. Sai liked his look, and thought that with his similar complexion and body type, he could pull them off.

But no matter how on-trend Sai's clothing looked, it didn't take him off the bullies' hit list. If anything, it painted a brighter target on his chest.

Sai threw on a T-shirt and left his bloody shirt soaking in the sink. He walked to his room and powered up his computer, then his window-box air conditioner. It was hot in Savannah, as usual. The humidity was the killer. Sai needed an escape from it, and the thought of his room soon turning into an icebox brought a smile to his face.

He sat down in front of his computer. At least he had SWARM to back him up. No matter how bad the day was, Drone Academy was his safe spot, his home away from his problems at home.

Under the active members' tab, Sai saw only two people, FlightFest and AndrewK. They were chatting in an open IM. Without hesitating, Sai joined the conversation.

It was the last time all three of them would ever speak together.

* * *

Today

Sai had watched the video three times so far, but he still didn't have any answers. At the start of the twenty-minute clip, which had been uploaded and shared from his account, Solo was visible in front of a mirror outside some store. Sai didn't recognize the place at all.

He paused the feed and studied the little white drone carefully. It was Solo, all right. Everything from the white blades to the cell phone center was identical. It was even the same make and model as Sai's phone — same color, same screensaver.

But Sai *knew* he hadn't taken Solo out yesterday. None of this made sense.

Of course, that wasn't the worst part. The worst part was the end of the video. Solo got so close to the young woman hanging from that cliff that the beads of sweat on her forehead were visible. So was the look of fear in her eyes. It was horrifying.

Then, after watching her hands slip down that root inch by inch, Solo just turned and flew away. The feed ended inexplicably.

Sai had looked up Eileen Wu after his first viewing of the video. It came as some relief that she had survived. Right after Solo had flown away, the rescue helicopter had returned. An emergency worker had lowered from the chopper using a line and hoist and secured Eileen to it somehow. The article wasn't very clear on that point. But either way, when the chopper flew off, a terrified Eileen Wu was safely inside it.

She was fine, at least physically. After scanning a few more Internet articles, Sai had learned that Eileen had spent the night in the hospital. She'd spent her time there crying uncontrollably. The whole event had really messed her up. *Solo* had messed her up.

But it couldn't have been Sai's drone. He was sure of it. Solo had been home when he'd gotten back from the party. And the drone was still fully charged. The most definite piece of evidence? Sai had been carrying his cell phone with him the whole time he'd been gone.

Either the video was a fake or the little white drone was. And based on the many, many news stories, Sai put his faith in the latter.

CHAPTER 41

THE TURN OF A KEY

Today

saiguy: *It wasn't me, you guys.*

Zor_elle: *Convince us.*

saiguy: *First off, it's a little upsetting you would even accuse me of that kind of piloting.*

saiguy: *Second, I had my phone with me the whole time. Ask Howard. I sent him that photo of my cousin's birthday party.*

ParkourSisters: *HowTo?*

HowTo: *Oh, yeah . . . the gif of the mouse shaking uncontrollably. That was hilarious.*

ParkourSisters: *And you didn't put two and two together?*

HowTo: *I'm just a mortal man, Parker. I can't always be the genius in the group.*

ParkourSisters: *I think you meant, "ever."*

saiguy: *So you guys believe me now?*

Zor_elle: *Just one question. Are you piloting Solo right now?*

saiguy: *No, I'm talking to you.*

Zor_elle: *Then I suggest you launch him right this second, and get your drone over to downtown Savannah.*

saiguy: *Why?*

Zor_elle: *Because according to the news, Solo is already there.*

* * *

Sai fished in his pocket for his keys. He was in such a hurry that it took him three tries before he finally managed to grab them. He slid his key into his closet door.

His father hated that closet. He hated Sai having secrets from him. After Sai's mom had left, back when Sai was just three years old, his dad had lost all sense of trust in anyone other than Mr. Morris. It often seemed like Sai's dad trusted their neighbor more than his own son.

But over the years, Sai had imparted to his father how important a little privacy was to a teenager. The fact that Sai had this secret closet at all was a testament to how far his dad had come.

The door unlocked with a click. Sai swung it open and looked at his most prized possession. There was Solo, sitting on the middle shelf, just as Sai had left him. Next to Solo were Sai's matching white virtual-reality goggles and gloves.

The drone and the VR equipment were immaculate. Sai kept his gear spotless and in perfect working order.

Even though he didn't talk to anyone outside of his fellow SWARM members about his piloting hobby, certainly not his dad or Mr. Morris, Sai felt a clean drone reflected on its owner. He was stylish and neat. Therefore his drone had to be the same.

Sai opened the window of his bedroom. Then he took his cell phone and plugged it into Solo's empty chamber. He put on his VR helmet and slid the bulky white gloves over his hands.

Both pieces of equipment had been heavily modified. The gloves were like something from the future. They could serve as remote controls, type on Sai's computer from a distance, or even record audio notes if he was in the mood to dictate.

Sai pulled the microphone down from the headset. As dramatically as possible, he spoke the word, "Launch."

Just like that, Solo came to life. The phone lit up with Sai's bright-white screensaver. The word *Solo,* in a matching font to the SWARM website's logo, appeared on the screen. The four blades spun into a blur, and within seconds, Solo hovered out of the closet.

Gesturing with his hands, Sai steered Solo out of his window. Once the drone was clear of the neighbor's tree and its hanging moss, Sai smiled. This was the fun part.

Unlike the rest of the SWARM drones, Solo was built for speed. Sai earned a fairly substantial allowance from his father, and, when combined with the money he made tutoring other students and mowing Mr. Morris's lawn, it made for a fairly steady and lucrative income. Every cent Sai earned went into one of two things: his wardrobe or his drone. Both were pretty impressive at this point.

Sai double-tapped a button on his right wrist. Then he watched through his goggles as Solo picked up speed. The speedometer readout in the corner of the virtual screen climbed from ten to twenty to forty to sixty miles per hour.

Sai didn't want to push Solo much faster than that tonight. He thought he could get it up to seventy, but he wasn't sure if it was practical. And he only had to travel about fifteen minutes at his current speed anyway. His house wasn't that far from downtown Savannah.

After ten minutes, Sai could already see the smoke.

CHAPTER 42

ZERO TO SEVENTY

Six months ago

saiguy: *Dude, that kind of joke is messed up.*

FlightFest: *You don't know my family's history, Andrew. I don't find jokes about mental illness funny.*

AndrewK: *Uh-oh. Don't go getting mad — it'd be a shame if we had to put you in the crazy house too.*

Sai couldn't believe what he was reading. This was SWARM. This was supposed to be a safe haven for people like FlightFest, aka Mark Warren. And here Sai was, not ten minutes after wiping blood off his face, dealing with a bully of a different nature. And this was almost worse — it was a member of Drone Academy.

He opened a new IM window and sent Mark a message.

saiguy: *I took a screenshot. Let's leave the site for today.*

FlightFest: *You saw what he said to me?!?*

saiguy: *Yeah, I saw.*

FlightFest: *You don't talk to people like that. Not your friends. Not anyone. You know what happened to my mom.*

saiguy: *I know. I'm sorry, Mark. I'm gonna call a group meeting.*

Mark didn't answer. He'd already logged off the SWARM website. Sai sat in his chair, chomping hard on his gum.

* * *

Today

Sai could see everything through the camera on his phone. The smoke was thick near the waterfront, so that was where he was headed.

"Sai?" said a familiar voice in his ear.

"Hey, Zora," said Sai.

"Can you talk?" she asked.

"Yeah," said Sai. He spit out his gum so his voice was clearer. "Got my VR set on. What's one more distraction?"

"How close is Solo? The news is only reporting one drone."

"Just a few blocks away," said Sai. "You want to give me the rundown?"

"OK, there are firefighters on the scene. Looks like they got everyone out of the building. But this little white drone —"

"The one that looks just like Solo."

"Yeah, the one that looks just like Solo," Zora confirmed. "It keeps buzzing the rescue workers. It almost knocked a firefighter right off his ladder."

"That's nuts."

"I know, right?"

"I'm closer now," said Sai, concentrating on the display projected in the goggles in front of his face. "I can see the building and . . . and there's that firefighter on his ladder."

"Send me your feed?" Zora asked. Sai pushed a few buttons on his left glove, and soon Zora was seeing the same view he was, albeit a few states removed.

On his monitor, Sai could see Solo's point of view. He watched as the drone zipped around the corner near the famous Savannah riverfront. The fire was blazing in what appeared to be a candle shop. There wasn't much doubt about how a fire could have started there, but the fire's origin wasn't his concern. Solo couldn't do anything to help on that front. What concerned Sai was the imposter drone busy making things worse. The Copycat.

"I see him!" Sai shouted into his headset's microphone. He was worked up now. Not only did he have to worry about flying Solo, but his reputation was on the line. Square in the center of his view was Copycat. It was currently buzzing close to the firefighter's head.

The firefighter swatted at the drone, trying to knock it out of the sky. Sai watched as the man nearly lost his balance on the ladder, steadying himself at the last possible moment.

"Me too," said Zora, sounding only slightly calmer. "So what now?"

They had found the doppelgänger. Everyone at SWARM would know that Sai was innocent. But that wasn't going to be enough. They had only located the problem. They hadn't dealt with it. There was still the question of *why* this was happening. Why was this guy messing with Sai in particular? What had he done to deserve this sort of personal attack?

"I'm gonna . . . I'm gonna try and ram it," said Sai.

"You're going to totally end Solo," said Zora.

"As long as I take out Copycat too, I'm good," Sai said. He sounded much more serious than usual.

Sai waited until the imposter drone had finished buzzing past the firefighter. The last thing he wanted to do was endanger any rescue workers. When the other drone was far enough away, it began to circle around, almost as if it was it was heading back for another pass at the fireman. That's when Sai acted.

Using both hands, Sai gestured forward like he was performing some sort of double karate chop. Solo instantly responded, picking up speed and heading directly for Copycat.

Sai took a deep breath, preparing for what was to come. Preparing to lose his best friend. When Copycat dove dramatically out of Solo's way, Sai didn't know whether to feel disappointment or relief.

There was no time to feel much of either. Sai reacted quickly, following Copycat down. When the imposter fled from the scene, Sai was right behind him.

The two drones cruised through the heavy Savannah air. Copycat swooped toward a street lamp. Solo followed, turning sideways to dodge a power line. Copycat increased his speed. Solo did the same.

"He's trying to lose you," said Zora, as if that fact had somehow been lost on Sai.

"Yeah, I got that," Sai said. He looked at the speedometer with the corner of his eye. Fifty miles per hour. Fifty-five mph. Sixty mph.

"How can you not catch him?" asked Zora, sounding frustrated. "Solo is like crazy fast!"

"It's . . ." Sai started, "it's more powerful than Solo. Not sure how he customized it to move like that."

Sixty-five mph. Sixty-six mph.

"You're going to burn out your drone," said Zora. Her voice had gone from somewhat annoyed to genuinely concerned.

"I'm almost on him," said Sai.

Solo raced after Copycat. They were high enough now that no obstacles stood in their way.

Sixty-seven mph. Sixty-eight mph.

"Sai!" Zora yelled.

Sixty-nine mph. Solo was so close to Copycat they were almost touching.

Then there was a flicker on Sai's goggles. Suddenly the view changed completely. Solo wasn't whizzing through the air right on Copycat's tail. He was facing the complete opposite direction.

"What's going on?" Zora half-shouted.

"I don't know . . . I . . ."

"What?"

Sai let out a frustrated sigh. "I burnt him out."

"I hate to say I told you so, but . . ."

Sai shook his head angrily. "I thought I could catch Copycat. I must have asked too much of Solo. Depleted his power. He couldn't handle that speed for that long."

"But I can see his feed," said Zora. "Looks like he's still operational."

"He's heading back home to his charging station," said Sai. "The automatic return feature activates when he needs to recharge."

"And we still don't know anything about this Copycat."

Sai didn't answer. He'd already run out of things to say. He just wanted to hang up and wait for his drone. And so he did.

CHAPTER 43

JUST ENOUGH SELF-REFLECTION

Today

HowTo: *Hey, man, what gives?*

saiguy: *Listen, I'm kind of busy.*

HowTo: *You're just hanging up on Zora now?*

saiguy: *Oh. Sorry about that. That was jerky.*

HowTo: *Don't say it to me, tell Zora.*

saiguy: *Later, OK?*

HowTo: *What's going on, Sai?*

saiguy: *I was just . . . I don't understand why someone is doing this. It feels so personal. Why is someone trying to mess with me specifically?*

HowTo: *That's the question, right? It's got to be someone who knows about Solo. How many people fit that bill?*

saiguy: *Just my dad and SWARM. And you four wouldn't —*

HowTo: *No, we wouldn't. But there weren't always just four.*

saiguy: *Oh, man. It's so obvious. AndrewK.*

HowTo: *Uh-huh.*

saiguy: *But even he wouldn't . . . do you think he'd go this far just to get back at me?*

HowTo: *Well, I mean, you did have him thrown out of SWARM . . .*

saiguy: *Hey, we all voted. It wasn't just me.*

HowTo: *I get that. I do. The question is, does AndrewK?*

* * *

Sai was having trouble looking up AndrewK's address. Unlike most of the other members of SWARM, AndrewK had never divulged his last name. K wasn't that specific, so Sai was left to play detective, looking through old transcripts from the SWARM message boards.

It had been nearly six months since they'd kicked AndrewK out of SWARM. He was a loudmouth who had been a bit rude to every member at one point or another, but Sai had always chalked up his behavior to Internet bravado.

Andrew had spent a lot of time on the SWARM boards, and Sai had always assumed there was a reason for that. He was probably in the same boat as the rest of the members. Andrew likely lashed out because he was bullied at school, or worse, at home. Sai could understand where he was coming from.

But there was no excuse for how Andrew had treated Mark all those months ago. Andrew knew about Mark's family history. And yet he'd gone ahead and made that joke anyway. The group had voted, and AndrewK was given a lifetime ban from the SWARM site.

But the damage had taken its toll. Mark had quit the group even before Andrew received his punishment, as did two other members, Jake — Joltin_Jake — and Trina — DroneOn.

Sai hadn't been particularly close to any of them back in those early days of Drone Academy. He'd never gotten to know Jake, Trina, or Mark on the same level as Zora, Howard, and Parker. He'd known Andrew the best of that bunch, though, so this betrayal definitely hurt.

Sai was so engrossed in past message board conversations that when his phone rang, he almost didn't check it. He looked over at its display — Zora. Then he looked at his finger. He had twisted his piece of gum completely around it, even though the other end was still held firmly between his teeth. His habit seemed to be getting worse by the day.

He picked up his phone. "Hey," he said. Before she had a chance to say anything, he continued, "Sorry I ran out on you like that. You know how I can get on the phone."

"I know you hate the phone," said Zora. Sai was relieved. She didn't sound angry.

"So that's why you called me."

"Exactly."

Sai smiled. "So what's up?" he asked.

"If I'm right, you're digging into old SWARM conversations, trying to find out anything you can about AndrewK."

"Yep," said Sai.

"I might have something that could help with that," Zora said.

As if on cue, Sai's computer gave out a quiet *blip*. He had a new email. He checked his account and discovered a photo of a black-and-red drone.

"That's Andrew's drone," Sai said. "I remember when he posted that. Said he got some custom work done."

"Right, but really look at the picture," Zora said.

Sai examined it. He enlarged the photo a bit using a zoom shortcut command on his keyboard. There was the drone, sitting on the floor of some generic apartment. No clues there. It was just gray carpet, light-brown walls, a white door with a mirror on the back . . .

And then he saw it. In the reflection was a Caucasian boy with red hair wearing a Cincinnati Reds baseball jersey.

"That's a face and a location," said Sai. "You are officially my new favorite person."

"Uh-huh," said Zora. "I know."

Sai couldn't see her face, but he wondered if Zora was smiling as large as he was.

CHAPTER 44

AIR TRAFFIC CONTROL

Today

ParkourSisters: *OK, so I used a bit of facial recognition software that's not exactly legal in all fifty states, but I found something.*

HowTo: *Which states?*

ParkourSisters: *What now?*

HowTo: *Which states is it illegal in?*

ParkourSisters: *All fifty. Aren't you paying attention?*

saiguy: *What did you find out, Parker?*

ParkourSisters: *I did a sweep of social media and found our guy. His name is Andrew Kraemer. He lives in Cincinnati with his dad, Aaron, his mom, Angela, and his older brother, Alex.*

saiguy: *Whoa!*

ParkourSisters: *I know, right? I guess his family has a thing for A names.*

saiguy: *Parker, you're a genius.*

ParkourSisters: *And an all-around athlete and loyal friend. Not to toot my own horn.*

HowTo: *When Parker is done tooting, let's talk about next steps.*

saiguy: *But wait, I don't get it. He lives in Ohio, but his drone was in Savannah?*

ParkourSisters: *Maybe he was on vacation or something?*

Zor_elle: *Maybe he still is.*

ParkourSisters: *Hey, Zora. When did you get here?*

Zor_elle: *Just now. And just in time, apparently. Check the local news for Savannah. A drone is causing a lockdown at the airport.*

saiguy: *Let me guess, it looks just like Solo.*

ParkourSisters: *And they say I'm the genius.*

* * *

Solo was close. Just a few more minutes, and he'd arrive at the Savannah/Hilton Head airport parking lot. Sai was glad he'd had time to fully recharge his drone. This mission was going to take as much battery life as he could get.

"You in position?" Zora's voice asked in his ear.

"Almost," said Sai. While the other SWARM members might complain about it, Sai enjoyed piloting Solo at night. The sun had set on the way over to the airport, and it was just now getting dark.

Sai had adjusted Solo's cell phone home screen from its usual bright white image to a black one. The last thing he needed right now was to be spotted by the local law enforcement and mistaken for Copycat. After all, Solo carried Sai's cell phone. He wouldn't be even remotely hard to track.

A moment later, Solo cruised above the parking lot. Sai looked around using his VR goggles. He saw a large truck near the front of the lot and hovered Solo close, then landed the drone gently on the truck's roof. Now was the hard part — the waiting.

"What do you see?" Sai asked.

"So I'm watching three different live coverage feeds at the airport. Copycat is flying above the terminal now. It looks like police are going to shoot it down."

"It shouldn't be long now," said Sai.

"Yeah, he's not going to want to stick around for this kind of heat," said Zora.

Neither spoke for a few minutes. Sai was lost in thought, remembering the early days of SWARM. His mind kept drifting back to that time whether he wanted it to or not.

Zora's voice snapped him back to attention. "OK!" she said, excitement in her voice. "This is it! He's making a run for it!"

Sai raised Solo up, just an inch or two from the truck's roof. He slowly rotated his drone, looking for any sign of Copycat. When a white blur flew overhead, Sai held his breath. This was it.

"Not too close," said Zora.

Sai knew she was right. He couldn't let Copycat see Solo. Who knew how long AndrewK would be in town? This was very likely Sai's only chance.

Solo began to rise into the air. Then, controlled by a two-handed gesture miles away, the little white drone sped forward, following his doppelgänger.

CHAPTER 45

FOLLOWING THE TRAIL

Today

"Who is this?" Andrew Kraemer asked, sounding confused. Which, to be fair, he probably was. He had never heard any of the SWARM members' voices in real life.

"Who do you think this is, Copycat?"

"I don't know," said Andrew. "That's why I asked."

"We know what you're doing, and we want you to stop," said Parker in her toughest voice. It didn't sound very imposing, despite her effort.

"Who is this?" Andrew asked again.

"I want you to know, I have no problem with going to the authorities. What you're doing is against the law," Parker continued.

"I'm going to hang up now," said Andrew.

"Wait," Howard interjected. "This is HowTo."

"Wh . . . HowTo?" said Andrew. "Seriously?"

"Oh, he's serious," said Parker. "Serious as a heart attack."

"All right, Parkour," said Howard, careful not to use Parker's real name. "He gets the idea. You're tough as nails."

"ParkourSisters?" said Andrew. "I haven't talked to you guys in forever. How did you get my number?"

"I have my ways," said Parker.

"Oookay," said Andrew. "So, what's up?"

"We could ask you the same thing," said Parker.

"Right . . ." said Andrew. "Well, I'm still flying my drone, but I've upgraded since the SWARM days —"

"To a little white model," interrupted Parker. It wasn't a question.

"Uh . . . no," said Andrew. "Mine's a custom job. It's canary yellow. Got six blades on it, which really helps get some height and —"

"How long have you been in Savannah?" Parker interrupted again.

"I'm sorry," said Andrew. "Could someone please tell me what we're talking about here?"

* * *

Six months ago

saiguy: *Hey, I just wanted to touch base again.*
FlightFest: *Hey.*

saiguy: *I called a group meeting, and we'll all be voting on whether to keep AndrewK in or not. I just wanted to see how you were feeling about all this.*

FlightFest: *Really? I'd think it would be obvious.*

saiguy: *So you want to kick him out?*

FlightFest: *Of course I want to kick him out. I want to do more than just kick him.*

FlightFest: *If I ever see that guy, I'm gonna mess him up bad. That's what I want to do.*

saiguy: *Come on, I mean yeah, he shouldn't have said what he said, but that's no reason to get violent. That's worse than what he did in the first place.*

FlightFest: *So you're taking his side?*

saiguy: *No. Not at all. I'm going to vote him out. I guess I just feel bad, you know? I know how much SWARM means to him and . . . I don't know.*

saiguy: *I'm not sure what I'm trying to say. My dad says I'm too sympathetic sometimes.*

saiguy: *FlightFest?*

saiguy: *Mark?*

saiguy: *Hello?*

* * *

Today

"How you doing on battery?" asked Zora. It was the first time she or Sai had spoken in the past five minutes.

"Getting low, but not low enough to activate the automatic return function," said Sai.

"Good," said Zora. "Who knows how long this is going to take."

"Hey, feel free to log off," said Sai. "Seriously. This could be a while, and there's no reason for both of us to have to tail this guy."

"I might do that," said Zora. "I've got a history test to cram for, and as usual, I've put it off until the very last minute."

"No problem," said Sai. He was still standing in his room, wearing his VR gear. He was getting tired, but he wasn't about to stop now. He'd been following Copycat for almost forty minutes. "I'll let you know if anything changes."

"Speak of the devil," said Zora.

"Hmm?" said Sai. He hadn't noticed it at first. Copycat had entered a steep dive. After a few seconds, Sai instructed Solo to do the same. Now they were finally getting somewhere.

Copycat approached a row of townhouses on a short suburban street. The drone flew to the corner building and then around to the back.

"Doesn't look like a hotel," said Zora.

"Could be a time-share," said Sai.

"Maybe . . ."

The doppelgänger drone landed in the backyard. Sai was careful not to do the same. Instead, he steered Solo toward the roof and landed his own drone softly near its rain gutter.

Suddenly, the back porch light turned on. The backyard lit up in a white glow.

"Ready to see our old friend Andrew again?" asked Zora.

"Not really," said Sai.

But it turned out, he wouldn't have to. A teenage boy walked out onto the lawn behind the house. He picked up Copycat, popped out its phone, and put it in his pocket. Then he turned to head back inside. Suddenly, he stopped. He looked up at the roof.

"We're spotted," said Zora.

Sai studied the young man looking up at him. The boy was certainly not the redhead he'd glimpsed in the mirror in that old photo from the SWARM boards. This boy had hair as black as Sai's own. His complexion didn't match, either. This guy was Asian. This was not Andrew Kraemer.

"Yeah, we've been spotted," Sai said. "But by who?"

CHAPTER 46

CATCHING UP WITH ANDREW

Today

"Wait," said Howard. "Is this a cell phone?"

"No," said Andrew. "This is my home number. Why?"

"So you're in Ohio as we speak?" asked Howard.

"Yeah?" said Andrew. "Wait, how do you know where I live?"

"We have our ways," said Parker.

"Park . . . Parkour," said Howard. "Andrew is in Ohio right now."

"Oh, snap," said Parker.

"Seriously," said Andrew. "What are you guys talking about?"

"So you're not on vacation?" asked Parker.

"I'm in my bedroom trying to play some Xbox," said Andrew. "But since you creeps are keeping tabs on me, you probably already know that."

"Our ways aren't that good —" Parker started to say.

"This is not our guy," Howard interrupted. "It can't be him."

"Still lost," said Andrew.

"Listen, Andrew," said Howard. "I'm sorry to take up your time. We've gotta go."

"Hey, man," said Andrew. "Whatever this is about, I just want to say, I'm really sorry for what I did. Back on the SWARM boards, you know. It was stupid. I was trying to be funny, and I said something really dumb."

"Yeah," said Howard. "OK, man. Take care."

"You too," said Andrew. "And say sorry to FlightFest for me, OK? I'd do it myself, but he blocked my email a few months back."

"We'll pass on the message if we talk to him," said Howard.

"What do you mean *if* you talk to him?" asked Andrew. "I thought he was still a mem—"

But Andrew didn't get to finish his sentence. Parker had already hung up on him.

* * *

"Andrew's not the bad guy!" Parker shouted after she'd established a conference call between all four SWARM members. "Well, I mean, he's *kind* of a bad guy in general, but he's not the one we're looking for specifically."

"Yeah," said Sai. "We know."

"Unless Andrew got some serious facial reconstruction surgery, he's not the drone's owner," said Zora.

"So you saw the drone's pilot?" Howard asked. "Tailing him worked?"

"Yep," said Sai. "We know where he lives. We already called the cops and reported him. We just have no idea *who* we reported."

"So what now?" asked Parker. "Case closed?"

"I don't know," said Sai. "I've got Solo coming home. It's gonna take a while. This kid lives all the way in Hinesville. That's like a forty-five-minute flight from my place. Solo's not even halfway home yet."

"I just keep wondering what his goal was," said Zora. "And how did he know everything about Sai's drone?"

"If it wasn't Andrew, then maybe someone else from SWARM?" Howard suggested. "It's got to be someone with enough computer savvy to hack Sai's YouTube account. And someone with expert piloting skills who's had access to our message boards. I mean, where else would he have even seen Sai's drone in the first place?"

Once again lost in thought, Sai didn't answer. He looked at his drone's live-camera feed through his VR goggles. He wasn't controlling Solo at the moment. The drone was simply following a return home command and didn't need him to pilot.

Sai no longer felt the rush he did when he was steering Solo. Watching his live feed now was just like watching a movie, albeit one with amazing depth added from his top-of-the-line virtual-reality goggles.

The problem was, the best movies had a twist at the end. And Sai's feed apparently didn't want to be left out.

"Whoa!" said Zora. She had been watching Solo's camera feed from her laptop at home. "Sai!"

"I see it," said Sai. "This is bad."

"What?" asked Parker. "Howard and I aren't linked up. What's happening?"

Sai didn't answer. He was already in the process of logging off the SWARM site.

Zora spoke for him. "It's Solo," she said. "He just crashed."

CHAPTER 47

THE HIGHWAY IS FOR FLYING

Today

At nearly sixteen years old, Sai felt like he was on the verge of a lot of things. He was old enough to work as a tutor but not old enough to get a job at the local mall. He was old enough to set his own bedtime at home but not old enough to stay out past his eleven o'clock curfew. He was old enough to have a learner's permit but not old enough to drive a car by himself.

So if he was going to rescue Solo, he'd need a partner in crime. And there was no one he could think of who enjoyed a good outing better than his neighbor, Mr. Morris.

Sai's finger pressed the doorbell on the house next door for the second time. It was only nine o'clock. Surely old people didn't go to bed this early.

He pressed the button again. If Mr. Morris didn't answer, Sai might have to make up some excuse and get his dad to take him. But then he'd have to answer a few dozen questions he didn't feel like answering. And that was if his dad wasn't feeling extra chatty.

His finger lingered over the doorbell, but he couldn't bring himself to press it again. Mr. Morris had probably been asleep in his recliner since seven-thirty. This was a lost cause.

But just as Sai turned to walk away, he heard the greeting.

"Hi, Sai," came the voice on the other side of the door's peephole. "What's up, guy?" Mr. Morris opened the front door.

"I need a favor," said Sai.

"Well, the doughnut shop's not open yet," said Mr. Morris. "And we've got two more days until Friday."

"Mr. Morris —"

"Maury."

"Mr. Morris, do you feel like going for a drive?"

* * *

"Holy cats, how fast you driving, kid?" Mr. Morris said from the passenger's seat.

"Oh, uh . . . I can slow down," said Sai. He honestly had no idea how fast he was going. He hadn't looked at the speedometer in minutes. Reluctantly he slowed Mr. Morris's car to the speed limit, although he couldn't really afford to.

They'd been driving for almost twenty minutes. Sai had a pretty good idea how his drone had crashed. It had been rammed by something behind it. That something could only be Copycat. Sai needed to get to Solo.

The crash had happened halfway between Sai's house and Hinesville. That meant that if Sai was rushing to the crash site from Savannah, there was a good chance that Copycat's pilot was rushing there from Hinesville. He probably had a head start too.

Sai had to make up the lost time any way he could. Without Sai meaning it to, the car's speedometer began to climb again.

"We must be going somewhere pretty important if you're in such a rush to get there," said Mr. Morris. He leaned his head back against the headrest. What little gray hair he had left clung to the fabric, drawn by static electricity.

"It's kind of complicated," said Sai.

"It always seems that way, doesn't it?" said Mr. Morris. "This the kind of problem you can solve by yourself? Or is this old-kook territory?"

"I think I can do it by myself."

"Well, if not, you got me for backup," said Mr. Morris. "I love a good round of fisticuffs."

"Really? Fisticuffs?"

"No, not really, you stick-in-the-mud. Even people my age don't say *fisticuffs* anymore."

Just then one of Sai's gloves beeped from the back seat. He nodded toward it. "That sound means we're getting close."

"What sound?"

"Never mind," said Sai. "There's a little GPS display on that control glove back there. Can you check it, and let me know when we get right over that red dot?"

"Will wonders never cease," said Mr. Morris as he retrieved the white VR glove from the back seat. "Let's see. You should have stopped . . . about three seconds ago."

Sai slammed on the brakes. Luckily, the interstate was empty, and there were no cars behind him. Otherwise, he'd be spending the better part of the year working to pay off the necessary repairs to the back of Mr. Morris's car.

Sai pulled over to the side of the road.

"Jeezy petes!" said Mr. Morris. "You're some driver."

"I gotta go see about something," said Sai. "I'll be right back. Stay here. Please."

Mr. Morris didn't answer. He just smiled his "boys will be boys" grin.

Sai left the car running as he grabbed his VR glove. Then he took off running down the side of the road, using the glove's display to light his way. A few yards away, he could see another similar glowing light.

Seconds later, Sai realized what it was. It was a glove, just like his, with a lit display, just like his. But this glove was residing on a very different arm.

CHAPTER 48

THE BOY IN THE DITCH

Today

"Hey!" Sai yelled at the shadowy person, who appeared to be standing over a ditch off the highway.

The figure didn't move. It froze in place, giving Sai the chance to jog a little closer. Now just five or six feet away from the mystery man, Sai could make him out.

It was the same teenager from the townhouse. He was holding both drones — Solo and Copycat — in his hands. Neither drone looked to be in working order.

Just seeing Solo like that made Sai cringe. It was like seeing a friend in the hospital. Hoping the mystery pilot wouldn't notice, Sai pressed a button on his own glove.

"Give me my drone," said Sai, trying to sound tough. His adrenaline was running high, but the truth was, this kid had a good foot on him in height and probably in width too.

Sai might be trendy, but muscular he wasn't. He didn't meet many kids his age who *weren't* bigger than him.

"It's out of commission," said the strange teen. "Don't you hate when that happens?"

"What's your problem?" Sai yelled. This had gone on long enough. He wasn't scared of this kid who had wrecked his drone. Not anymore, at least. He refused to be bullied.

"You're my problem, Sai."

"I don't even know who you are!"

"Seriously? I'm Mark, you self-involved jerk. FlightFest."

Sai opened his mouth but didn't say anything.

"What, you don't remember me?" said Mark. "I'm the guy whose side you *didn't* chose when AndrewK made fun of my family on the SWARM boards."

"That's . . . wait, what?" said Sai. He was really confused now. "I didn't pick his side. We threw Andrew off the boards. Like right away."

"He was still a member when I quit."

"Well, maybe you quit too fast."

"You defended him," said Mark. He seemed to be getting angrier now. "How do you not remember this? You said you felt bad for him. You felt bad for the bully. Do you know how many times that has happened to me?"

"I don't know anything about you."

"Well, I know a lot about you. For starters, that your passwords are ridiculously simple. You know that?"

Parker had warned Sai about that very thing. But Sai hadn't given it much thought. Apparently he should have.

"I just . . . it wasn't right, you getting to have your little secret society," Mark continued. "Meanwhile, I'm picked on at school, my dad's a complete jerk, my mom's dealing with her own issues, and then I get bullied on my own message boards?"

"You didn't have to quit," said Sai. "We fixed the problem."

"You didn't even realize what the problem *was*," said Mark. "So I shut Solo down. And he's just the first. I'm taking out SWARM, Sai. I know everything about you people, and you don't know jack about me."

"I know where you live. I called the police," said Sai.

"So what?" said Mark. "They think it was your drone, not mine. They don't know I uploaded the video. All I have to do is wipe our phones. All the evidence that's left points right to you."

"You're right," Sai said, shaking his head.

"So what?" said Mark. "You gonna fight me now? You gonna fight for your drone? Even I can take someone as tiny as you."

"You're right," Sai said again. "Have a good night, Mark."

Sai turned around and began walking back to Mr. Morris's car. He half expected Mark to slug him in the back of the head. But the punch never came. So Sai drove home. Besides, he already had exactly what he needed.

THERE'S NO SUCH THING AS ALONE

Today

". . . was your drone, not mine. They don't know I uploaded the video. All I have to do is wipe our phones. All the evidence that's left points right to you."

Sai pressed the pause button on the MP3 recording. His friends didn't need to hear any more. He chewed his gum and checked his IM.

ParkourSisters: *Man, I really need to get me some of your equipment, Sai. That stuff can do anything.*

saiguy: *It can do enough. I had the glove recording the whole time.*

HowTo: *I'm not a legal expert, but that's gotta be enough to incriminate him, right?*

saiguy: *I guess. I don't know. I'm heading to the police station in about an hour. I have to make an official statement.*

ParkourSisters: *This is great, right? We caught him. FlightFest is going down. He'll have to pay for the damages, replace your drone. The whole nine yards.*

saiguy: *Probably.*

ParkourSisters: *It's not just me, is it? Even though Sai's typing, we can all hear his sadness clear as day, right?*

HowTo: *Parker . . .*

Zor_elle: *What's going on, Sai?*

saiguy: *I don't know. It just doesn't feel like a win.*

Zor_elle: *Yeah, I get it. But it is. You did good, and maybe this whole thing will straighten Mark out.*

Zor_elle: *You've got a big heart, Sai. If someone else can't see that, that's their problem.*

saiguy: *Yeah, OK. Thanks, Zora. Listen guys, I gotta go.*

Logging off, Sai leaned back in his chair. He didn't feel like being in his room anymore. He walked downstairs and out the door. Mr. Morris was out near the street, getting his mail from the mailbox.

"Hi, Sai," his neighbor said. "What's up, guy?"

"Not much," said Sai.

"No more fightin' crime?" Mr. Morris asked.

"No," said Sai. He pulled at the gum in his mouth with his fingers. "Nothing like that."

"Good. Seems to me like you had a problem, and you handled it yourself," said Mr. Morris. "You know . . . solo."

Sai felt his gum roll back into his cheek. He lowered his hand. Mr. Morris was smiling at him. Sai smiled back.

"So, doughnuts tomorrow?" said Mr. Morris.

"Doughnuts tomorrow," Sai agreed.

On his way back upstairs, Sai felt like spitting his gum out into the kitchen trash can. And so he did.

* * *

One year ago

ParkourSisters: *This is awesome, you guys.*

Zor_elle: *I gotta side with Parkour on this one. Seriously cool logo.*

AndrewK: *Thanks again for setting this site up, saiguy.*

saiguy: *Hey, it was a group effort. I'm just glad I could help.*

DroneOn: *All right, well I'm gonna log off for tonight.*

Joltin_Jake: *Me too. Family reunion early tomorrow. Ugh.*

HowTo: *Ouch. Good luck with that. Signing out.*

AndrewK: *I'm out too.*

Zor_elle: *Night all.*

ParkourSisters: *Night.*

FlightFest: *I've got no plans. You want to hang out here for a bit?*

saiguy: *Sure, man. I've got time.*

FlightFest: *Cool. Sometimes I'm in no hurry to get back to the real world, you know?*

saiguy: *Hey, that's why we fly.*

FlightFest: *Yeah.*

FlightFest: *That's why we fly.*

About the Author

The author of the Amazon best-selling hardcover *Batman: A Visual History*, Matthew K. Manning has contributed to many comic books, including *Beware the Batman*, *Spider-Man Unlimited*, *Pirates of the Caribbean: Six Sea Shanties*, *Justice League Adventures*, *Looney Tunes*, and *Scooby-Doo, Where Are You?* When not writing comics themselves, Manning often authors books about comics, as well as a series of young reader books starring Superman, Batman, and the Flash for Capstone. He currently resides in Asheville, North Carolina, with his wife, Dorothy, and their two daughters, Lillian and Gwendolyn. Visit him online at www.matthewkmanning.com.